MW01138066

Seabreeze Inn and _Coral Cottage_ series

"A wonderful story… Will make you feel like the sea breeze is streaming through your hair." – Laura Bradbury, Bestselling Author

"A novel that gives fans of romantic sagas a compelling voice to follow." – _Booklist_

"An entertaining beach read with multi-generational context and humor." – _InD'Tale_ Magazine

"Wonderful characters and a sweet story." – Kellie Coates Gilbert, Bestselling Author

"A fun read that grabs you at the start." – Tina Sloan, Author and Award-Winning Actress

"Jan Moran is the queen of the epic romance." —Rebecca Forster, _USA Today_ Bestselling Author

"The women are intelligent and strong. At the core is a strong, close-knit family." — Betty's Reviews

The Chocolatier

"A delicious novel, makes you long for chocolate." – _Ciao Tutti_

"Smoothly written...full of intrigue, love, secrets, and romance." – *Lekker Lezen*

The Winemakers

"Readers will devour this page-turner as the mystery and passions spin out." – *Library Journal*

"As she did in *Scent of Triumph*, Moran weaves knowledge of wine and winemaking into this intense family drama." – *Booklist*

The Perfumer: Scent of Triumph

"Heartbreaking, evocative, and inspiring, this book is a powerful journey." – Allison Pataki, *NYT* Bestselling Author of *The Accidental Empress*

"A sweeping saga of one woman's journey through World War II and her unwillingness to give up even when faced with the toughest challenges." — Anita Abriel, Author of *The Light After the War*

"A captivating tale of love, determination and reinvention." — Karen Marin, Givenchy Paris

"A stylish, compelling story of a family. What sets this apart is the backdrop of perfumery that suffuses the story with the delicious aromas – a remarkable feat!" — Liz Trenow, *NYT* Bestselling Author of *The Forgotten Seamstress*

BOOKS BY JAN MORAN

Summer Beach Series

Seabreeze Inn

Seabreeze Summer

Seabreeze Sunset

Seabreeze Christmas

Seabreeze Wedding

Seabreeze Book Club

Seabreeze Shores

Seabreeze Reunion

Seabreeze Honeymoon

Seabreeze Gala

Seabreeze Library

Seabreeze Harvest

Coral Cottage Series

Coral Cottage

Coral Cafe

Coral Holiday

Coral Weddings

Coral Celebration

Coral Memories

A Very Coral Christmas

Crown Island Series

Beach View Lane

Sunshine Avenue

Orange Blossom Way

Hibiscus Heights

The Love, California Series

Flawless

Beauty Mark

Runway

Essence

Style

Sparkle

20th-Century Historical

Hepburn's Necklace

The Chocolatier

The Winemakers: A Novel of Wine and Secrets

The Perfumer: Scent of Triumph

Life is a Cabernet

JAN MORAN

SEABREEZE
Library

SEABREEZE LIBRARY

SUMMER BEACH, BOOK 11

JAN MORAN

SUNNY PALMS

PRESS

Library of Congress Cataloging-in-Publication Data
Moran, Jan.
/ by Jan Moran

ISBN 978-1-64778-189-7 (epub)
ISBN 978-1-64778-247-4 (paperback)
ISBN 978-1-64778-248-1 (hardcover)
ISBN 978-1-64778-249-8 (large print)
ISBN 978-1-64778-250-4 (audiobook)
ISBN 978-1-64778-336-5 (large print)

Published by Sunny Palms Press. Cover design by Okay Creations. Cover
images copyright Deposit Photos.

Sunny Palms Press
991 Lomas Santa Fe Dr. Suite C-113
Solana Beach, CA, USA 92075
www.sunnypalmspress.com
www.JanMoran.com

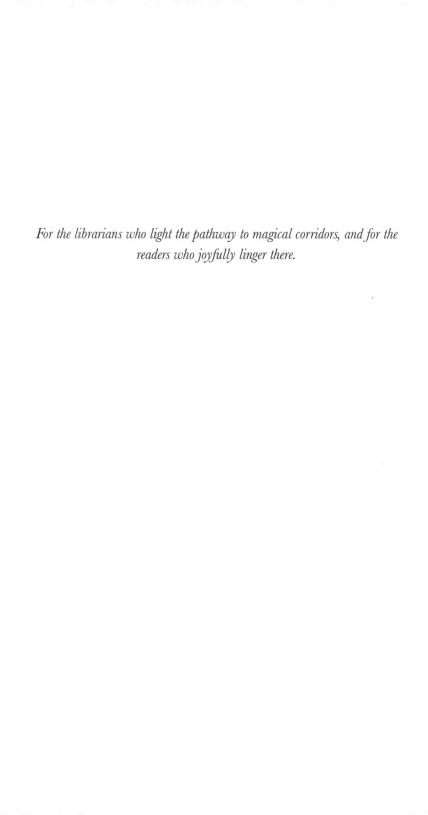

For the librarians who light the pathway to magical corridors, and for the readers who joyfully linger there.

1

I promise you'll be interested in this, Nan had told her, refusing to say anything else until Ivy arrived. She wondered what Nan had put aside for her at Antique Times in the village. Likely, it had to do with the renovation of the Seabreeze Inn. She'd been searching for vintage fixtures and parts for replacements.

Ivy walked toward the stucco façade ablaze with flaming pink bougainvillea flowers fluttering over the doorway. Once inside, the scent of lavender potpourri emanated from a crystal bowl warmed under a Victorian lamp.

Her friend looked up from the glass countertop she was cleaning.

"Hi, Nan. What treasures did you find for me?"

Nan hurried to greet her, her red curls fairly bobbing with excitement. "I have it right here." She opened an old scrapbook and pointed to a yellowed article. "Read that."

Ivy inclined her head. "But I thought you might have crystal doorknobs or light fixtures for me."

"Trust me, this is what you really want to see," Nan replied, tapping the article.

Her husband emerged from the office and greeted her. With his English accent and proclivity for Hawaiian shirts, Arthur was a delightful addition to Summer Beach. He gestured to the snipped column. "Go on, read it."

"Just a moment." Ivy couldn't imagine why they were staring at her with such rounded eyes. She brought her orange butterfly-print reading glasses from her straw tote and peered at the old article.

In an instant, she realized why they'd called her.

Her chest tightened, and she could hardly believe what she was reading. "Why have I never heard anything about this?" She looked up at the proprietors of the shop.

"Well, it was a long time ago," Nan replied. "That article is from early 1939."

"A century-ish ago now," Arthur added, his eyes sparkling behind his glasses. "It was another time, yet in many ways, not so very different from our own. People don't change much."

Nan clasped her hands. "They still love to read."

Ivy tucked her hair behind an ear and reread the short piece. "This reports that Amelia Erickson had plans to build a library here. What exactly did that mean?" Mildly frustrated, Ivy blew out a puff of air.

Why hadn't the journalist been more specific? Ideally, Ivy needed a location, plans, and a large bag of gold coins hidden under a mattress.

Arthur flipped through the old file of articles he and his wife had collected in their research on Summer Beach. "Amelia Erickson was quite civic-minded. Remember how she spoke of purchasing the defunct Seabreeze Shores Airfield?" He tapped an article. "It's right here. She planned to dedicate that land for a community park."

"And now it is," Ivy said. Not long ago, the residents of Summer Beach came together for that effort. "Does she mention a library in that piece?"

Arthur shook his smoothly shaven head. "Sadly, no."

A strange sense of energy sizzled through Ivy. She shivered slightly, even though it was a warm spring day in the small beach town. Yet, this feeling was also familiar, especially when she stumbled on one of Amelia Erickson's unfinished projects. The woman's presence still infused the old inn once known as Las Brisas del Mar, which had been her beach home. Everyone felt it, including her sister Shelly, their niece Poppy, and her daughters Sunny and Misty.

Occasionally, even guests.

Still, Ivy wasn't ready to admit that publicly, as that would brand the Seabreeze Inn as haunted. She had worked too hard to revive the old property her late husband intended for his mistress for people to fear visiting.

Nan touched Ivy's hand. "We thought you might like to know. Maybe you can sway the mayor with this information."

Ivy smiled at the idea. "I wish it worked like that, but my husband is committed to doing what's best for Summer Beach. That includes fiscal responsibility."

Arthur chuckled. "Indeed he does. I remember when Bennett blocked your application to turn the old house into a bed-and-breakfast."

Nan joined him in laughter. "It took a natural disaster to convince him that time. The two of you might never have fallen in love if he hadn't been forced to relocate to the inn after the fire."

"It was something like that," Ivy said, smiling. "I hope funding a new library doesn't take another disaster."

"Faulty wiring destroyed the old one," Arthur said, shaking his head.

That occurred late last year. Ivy had taken it upon herself to return the community's support of the inn by welcoming former library patrons to its public spaces. Meanwhile, she had been lobbying the city for a replacement library.

So far, she had failed, and that was a sore point between her and her husband. But she wasn't giving up.

"Everyone misses gathering at the library," Arthur said. "Small as it was, it was important to people of all ages. After all, what's a town without a library for books and news and a place to meet without the admission price of a cup of coffee?"

"You're a fine one to talk." Nan nudged him. "You're quite happy to go to Java Beach every morning. You and your gossiping cronies."

Arthur put his arm around his wife and squeezed her to him. "It's not like that, my pet. I'm performing a service for Summer Beach, listening to residents' concerns. I daresay you have the ear of the mayor, too."

"Excuse me?" Nan raised her brow in faux shock. "Not like Ivy does."

Though their midlife shenanigans were charming, Ivy cut in, grinning. "Okay, you two, that's enough. Sadly, I don't have any power over city matters."

During the week, Nan worked as the receptionist at City Hall. She had plenty of influence, too, but neither of them could conjure more funds in the budget to rebuild a library. The owner's property insurance in the library's leased space hadn't been enough, and the community couldn't make up the difference.

She turned back to the article about the library. "Are you sure this is the only mention of the project?"

"That's all we could find," Arthur replied. "By chance, might there be extra funds from the renovation project?"

Recently, Ivy held a gala fundraiser to restore the old property as a centerpiece of the community. "I'm afraid those finances are committed."

That's what Bennett said about the city budget, too.

"Well, then, do you still want the vintage wall sconces for the ballroom?" Nan asked, changing the subject. "They're such a good match to the ones you have. We were lucky to find them."

"Fortunately, those are in the budget," Ivy replied, nodding.

"We're always watching estate sales for you," Arthur said. "We know the effort it takes to keep up the older properties in town."

"I appreciate that." Another shiver touched Ivy's neck, and she rubbed it. "You'll let me know if you find anything else about Amelia Erickson's plan for a local library?"

"Of course," Nan replied, though her expression was doubtful. "And best of luck with your city council presentation tonight."

"Thanks. I'll need heaps of good fortune this time." Ivy smiled at the couple's genuine, heartfelt encouragement for her second attempt. She was leading this library proposal for the small town, and she hated to disappoint the kind people who had been there for her since she'd arrived when she was newly widowed, cash-poor, and in desperate need of a fresh start in life.

So many strangers-turned-friends had supported her efforts, sending friends and family to stay at the fledgling inn. Darla, the grouchy neighbor who'd once sued her, had become an ally. She was still nosy, but she meant well. Darla was especially fond of Ivy's brother-in-law, Mitch. Darla considered him a son.

Ivy paid for the sconces and left the shop to walk back to the inn, wondering what she might have overlooked. She had identified additional state grants and a small private donation. Would it be enough this time?

As she approached the old house, her heart tightened. If ever she needed some of Amelia Erickson's guidance, it was now.

"FINALLY, THIS IS THE LIFE." Ivy kicked off her sneakers in the vintage convertible as Bennett drove along the coastline. With the top down, the 1950s cherry-red Chevy was open to the clear blue sky, and she shook back her hair in the breeze.

She hadn't felt this relaxed since before her bid for a new library had been denied again at City Hall last week. That disappointment had become an undercurrent in their marriage, but she was trying to rise above it. As mayor, her husband had a duty to the city that had nothing to do with her.

At least, not usually.

Since sunrise, they'd been clearing guest rooms of furnishings, shifting boxes and furniture from one block of rooms to another in preparation for tomorrow's construction kickoff. She was physically drained, but in a good way.

Bennett rested an arm across the back of the bench seat. He caught a strand of her hair and twirled it. "We needed this little getaway. I'm sorry about the budget—"

"Let's not mention it. I know it's out of your control."

"You know I love you, and if it were within my power to give you what you wanted, I would."

"I know," she said softly. It seemed they couldn't do much about this project that was so close to her heart and many others in Summer Beach. "Can we start again?"

"Good idea." Exhaling, Bennett rested his hands on the

large steering wheel and lifted his chin toward the crashing waves they passed. "This view always makes me happy."

"Me, too." Feeling a measure of relief, she squeezed his knee through his jeans. However, just because they weren't going to talk about the library didn't mean she was abandoning the project.

With fresh resolve, she would strive to appreciate the small details in her life. She drew her hand back over the red leather seats. Bennett had spent months restoring this car, a labor of love he'd given her before they married.

Beside her, he flexed his fingers and rolled his neck. The salt-tinged breeze whisked away the dust and fatigue of the day, leaving only the anticipation of a beautiful sunset in its wake.

"We all worked hard today," he said. "Moving the furnishings would have taken longer if you hadn't had such an organized approach."

"You can thank Poppy for that." Her niece had invited family and friends and made a workday into a party. That was a brilliant idea, with the young, strong cousins all trying to outwork each other. Some were still there, proving themselves. The difference between being in her forties versus her twenties was that now she valued self-preservation.

In other words, she knew when to quit or take a break. Physically, anyway.

Massaging an aching arm, Ivy glanced out to sea, watching waves glimmer in the fading light. If only she could catch this precise moment in her artwork. She wouldn't have the time or space to devote to painting until the renovation was complete. Although her studio was sealed off, she had sketch books she could carry with her.

Turning back to Bennett, she said, "Let's take the rest of the night off. Reed's crew arrives early in the morning."

"You got it." Bennett turned the radio dial to an old pop rock station, and an old Beach Boys tune about good vibrations filled the air. He tapped the steering wheel to the beat. "Here's our vibe."

She snapped her fingers. "I love this song. Do you know how to play it?"

"It's been a while, but I can probably manage it," Bennett replied, a smile tugging his lips.

"The first time I ever saw you, you were playing a guitar on the beach. You have no idea how many times your soundtrack ran through my mind."

"And here we are again." Bennett slowed by a spot off the road where they had an unobstructed view of the horizon and turned off the ignition.

They were still dressed in worn jeans and T-shirts. Ivy's shirt bore traces of dust they'd disturbed, and Bennett had a smudge across one cheek she found endearing.

She leaned over to wipe it before kissing him and resting her head on his shoulder. The sun was sinking quickly toward the horizon. Just then, her stomach growled, and she laughed. "Didn't mean to spoil the moment."

Bennett put a hand to her stomach and grinned. "Can't have you riding on empty. Wait here."

He got out to open the trunk. When he returned, he was carrying their wicker basket, a thick moving blanket, and his guitar case.

"You're an angel. I didn't see you pack the car with a picnic."

He shook his head. "I'm not giving away my secrets."

Quickly, she climbed out to spread the blanket on the sand.

"I didn't want to let this day go by without celebrating." He knelt and produced a bottle of sparkling water with fresh lime wedges that he poured for them. Seagulls soared overhead, and he nodded up at them. "I brought a spread of food, but those are smart rascals. Shall I feed you?" He brought out a bunch of red grapes.

She remembered once when seagulls had swooped in to steal their sandwiches. "Would you peel them, too?"

Laughing, Bennett gave her a handful of grapes. "Don't press your luck."

"What else do you have tucked away in there?"

"You'll see." Next up were wedges of cheese and artisanal crackers.

Ivy sat beside him, pleasantly bewildered but enjoying this mini feast. "Are we celebrating the commencement of construction?"

"You don't know?"

"All I know is that you sure know how to sweep a lady off her feet."

"You'll remember in a moment." Bennett kissed her, then ran a piece of dark chocolate over her lips.

She closed her eyes. "Mmm, my favorite."

"Which one, this or me?"

"Both," she said, smiling. "More chocolate, please. Then you."

Teasing her, he pulled the chocolate chunk away, his eyes crinkling at the corners. "Do you remember yet?"

She flung her arms out. "I give up, totally and completely, to you."

He laughed. "It's our anniversary."

She bit into the bitter dark chocolate and looked at him quizzically. "Didn't we just celebrate that? Or has the year flown past, and the renovation is miraculously complete?"

They'd marked the occasion with a dinner at Beaches just a few weeks ago. Then, she burst into laughter. "This is the anniversary of our second marriage, isn't it?"

"Thanks to you. Double the pleasure."

She lobbed a grape at him. "If something is worth doing, it's worth doing twice."

"If that's what it takes, I'll gladly marry you twice a year for the rest of our lives," Bennett said, sealing that promise with a kiss.

She leaned against his shoulder, remembering how their first attempt at marriage had almost gone sideways because her out-of-state driver's license had expired. The county clerk made no exception, even if Bennett was a mayor.

With their family in attendance, they'd proceeded with a commitment ceremony on the beach, performed by Brother Rip, so named after his surfing handle, *riptide*. A gentle giant with braids past his shoulders, Brother Rip was a popular beach minister who held sunrise surfing services along the beaches.

Since this religious ceremony was their first, Ivy considered this with their family and friends as their wedding date for anniversary purposes.

Their legally binding marriage had come a little later after her updated identification arrived in the mail. It was only a formality, so she'd arrived in a simple white sundress at the Summer Beach City Hall for their quick ceremony during Bennett's lunch hour. Their families and friends had celebrated the first occasion with them, so they'd thought this was the easiest way to settle the outstanding legal issue.

Bennett's colleague in the building department, Boz, served as a witness, and Nan surprised them with a shower of rose petals. After sipping smoothies in the village, they returned to work. Later that evening, they enjoyed dinner on the patio at the Coral Cafe with friends.

"Most people have to wait years for their silver anniversary," Bennett said, refilling their flutes. "We'll get to it twice as fast. Twelve and a half years."

"I'm glad I married such a practical man."

Bennett's expression warmed. "Here's to the visionary woman who taught me to see beyond practicalities to what could be. I'm glad life brought around a second chance for us." He raised his glass and clinked hers. "To many more anniversaries. At least twice a year."

The sun touched the horizon as they kissed, bathing them in fiery splendor. Bennett pulled away. "So, my darling, what do you wish for this coming year?"

She hesitated. What she'd recently poured her heart into had been denied at City Hall, not that it was Bennett's fault. "A smooth, uncomplicated renovation is probably enough. No high drama, so we can reopen for business."

Why sour a lovely evening? Besides, the community didn't have the budget for a replacement library. She'd collected resident signatures and made a second plea to the city council, but there weren't enough funds to build and restock a library. Summer Beach was a small town. Many communities their size couldn't support a library either.

It was the loss for residents she still mourned. After all the townspeople had done for her and her family, she owed them a debt of gratitude. In her mind, a library would have the most meaning to them and their families.

"Are you still with me?" He took her hand and kissed it, drawing her attention back. "The renovation should be complete before summer."

Ivy nodded. "I better be, or we'll lose money on reservations."

He nodded in understanding and shooed away an encroaching seagull that seemed particularly insistent upon joining them. "You always find a way to make your dreams happen. Here's to not losing money or love."

"That last part will never happen." She smiled at him over the rim of her glass.

"Neither will the first part, even if we need to pick up hammers again. I will love you through it all, darling."

Sliding her hand around his neck, Ivy echoed his sentiment with a kiss. After a few moments of enjoying each other in their arms, Bennett brought out his guitar and began to play.

Listening to him strum his guitar, she inclined her head, recalling all that she and Shelly had done to make the old beach house habitable and turn it into a thriving business. Bennett arrived to help later when he and other locals sought shelter there after the fire. That was the beginning of their second chance in life.

When he paused, she asked, "What is your wish for the coming year?"

"That we remain as happy as we are this moment."

Ivy listened to her husband play, enjoying their time together. Tomorrow would bring the chaos of construction, with Reed and his crew tearing apart sections of the inn. The fundraising gala had made it all possible. But tonight was theirs. A private celebration while they could still find the time to be alone.

The uncomfortable undercurrent sparking between them dissipated. The library denial wasn't his fault, but still, she was frustrated with the process. Somehow, she would find a way to return a beloved institution to Summer Beach. She couldn't depend on Bennett, or rather, *the city*, to help much.

She nestled closer to her husband, pouring love into the fissures of their marriage to bond them forever. They needed that magical glue now because the next weeks ahead would test their patience more than ever.

2

"Watch your head," Ivy said to her sister as they stepped through the plastic sheeting that divided the music room from the hallway.

Shelly ducked through the zippered opening and into the room under renovation. Her long chestnut hair was piled into a messy bun. "This place is such a wreck. At least it's intentional this time. Remember when we took hammers to the old brick wall?"

"That moment changed everything." Ivy grinned as memories surged through her. The paintings they'd found sent news of their fledgling inn zinging through the art world, bringing the guests they desperately needed to keep the business afloat.

The inn would soon be completely closed. Her brother Forrest had fast-tracked the renovation and put his son Reed in charge.

Ivy peeled a piece of blue painter's tape from her sneaker and tossed it aside, brushing her hands on her worn jeans.

Most of their guests had checked out, except for one in the rear cottage and their long-term guest, Gilda.

The book clubs had also pleaded for one more meeting there. Reluctantly, Ivy relented. Since the Summer Beach library was damaged and closed, Ivy provided space for library patrons to meet at the inn.

Shelly sneezed from the dust. "This renovation is getting serious now."

"Reed's crew is working on electrical issues now," Ivy said. "Guests will be able to use hair dryers at the same time without blowing fuses." She grinned at a memory, although it hadn't been funny at the time. "Remember the Wilson wedding?"

"How could I forget?" Shelly made a face. "The ceremony was delayed so the bride and bridesmaids could dry their hair. That cost us a couple of free nights and extra appetizers while everyone waited."

A sense of relief coursed through Ivy. "Those incidents are nearly behind us."

"We'll have to find higher-class problems, like temperature control in my yoga space. Some guests complain it's too hot, but I tell them it's good for stretching." Shelly reached out and flicked a light switch several times. She nodded with satisfaction. "Look, no more flickering lights."

"Or midnight plumbing calls," Ivy added, reminiscing with a strange fondness for the old house's original dilapidated condition when they'd first seen it.

Shelly bumped Ivy's shoulder. "Just when I was getting good at plumbing emergencies. That's a life skill I finally sort of mastered. Does this mean I won't need my pipe wrench anymore?"

"Don't toss it just yet," Ivy replied. "I'm sure you could be on call for any number of folks in town. There's always Darla." Ivy jerked her head toward their neighbor's home.

"I didn't say I wanted to do it, only that I can." Shelly laughed. "Mitch appreciates it, though. He's better in the kitchen, so we balance each other. His customers at Java Beach don't care if he can't handle a hammer as long as he can work that fancy espresso machine and whip up breakfast."

Ivy gazed around the room, pleased with the progress. Construction would shift into an even higher gear after the last guest checked out in a few days. The sooner they finished, the sooner they could reopen for the high summer season.

A good-looking younger man wearing work clothes and boots stepped through the plastic sheeting. "What do you think, Aunt Ivy?"

"You and your crew are doing a beautiful job, Reed, but…" She bit her lip, hating to bother him again, but a guest had complained. "It's Dr. Kemper in room 114. Could your crew begin later in that section? Or work more quietly?"

"I told you we shouldn't have rented any rooms," Shelly said, shaking her head. "It's not like me to turn down the money, but this place is a wreck. I wouldn't stay here."

"It was good enough for you for a long time," Ivy said, nudging her.

Shelly grinned and poked her back. "You know what I mean."

Ivy shook her head at her sister, although she wasn't upset. Shelly was being her usual contrarian self, and Ivy had learned to laugh at most of her comments and antics. At least, she tried.

As for Dr. Meryl Kempner, the woman had arrived for her granddaughter's birthday and found there were no other options in town. Her family members had taken every available room and couch at her son's home. After one night on a small air mattress, she'd pleaded with Ivy, citing her aching back from an injury sustained during her military service.

Ivy was friends with the family, so she readily agreed to accommodate the retired woman.

Reed stroked his chin. "How about we work on another part of the house in the mornings?"

"That would be great," Ivy replied. Her nephew had accommodated their guests as they wound down the reservations.

"Our visitors will only be here through the weekend," she added. "We have no more bookings after that." They had sent many guests to the Seal Cove Inn. Others had delayed their visits.

Ivy thought renting rooms in the rear cottage, which once housed the housekeeping staff, would be alright since they were on the other side of the pool.

Yet, the noise in rooms was still plenty loud.

After discussing the work Reed's crew needed to do in this room, they threaded their way through the hallway. The floors were covered in paper to protect the wooden floors before refinishing.

"I'm sorry about the noise," Reed said. "Were you disturbed, Aunt Ivy?"

"We're early risers. Bennett was already on the beach for his morning run." Ivy and her husband made their home in the old chauffeur's apartment above the garages near the other cottage rooms. Although Reed's early morning footsteps woke her, she gave him a reassuring smile. "The work has to be done."

The hundred-year-old inn, once owned by art collectors Amelia and Gustav Erickson, was long overdue for a restoration. Thanks to her friend Viola in San Francisco, who lived in the Erickson's former primary home, a mansion in Pacific

Heights, their fundraiser for the repair and community preservation had been phenomenally successful. Viola's friends had turned out to support her cause.

Ivy also had enough savings to update some furnishings for guest and community rooms.

They should finish just in time for the high season.

As they entered the foyer, Poppy looked up from the front desk. "We just had a call for another reservation. When I suggested she call the other inn, the woman told me she'd tried. With our referrals, the Seal Cove Inn is full now. But this woman is persistent. I explained the construction situation, and she seemed okay with it. She said she can sleep through anything."

Ivy had heard that one before, but it wasn't always true. "We had planned on closing during this phase." Even as she spoke, a distant memory tickled her mind.

"I know, but she seems eager to stay here," Poppy said, pulling her silky blond hair into a ponytail as she spoke. "She's been following Shelly's blog and social posts about the inn for a long time. I thought we could make an exception, just for the weekend."

"I don't know," Ivy said. Aside from the noise, she was concerned about the potential liability. What if a guest tripped over an electrical cord? Ivy had impressed upon Dr. Kempner the need for caution, showing her the safe areas to walk.

"I thought we could put her near our other guest," Poppy said. "Besides, Reed and his crew won't work on the weekend."

Reed looked skeptical. "We are now if we want to make the deadline before summer."

"Surely she can find something nearby," Shelly said with a dismissive wave. "Even though I'm flattered she's been following me."

A guilty look washed over Poppy's face as she turned to Ivy.

"The problem is, she's not far away. I've already booked her into a room. You told me to embrace decision-making, so I did."

"Then let's welcome her," Ivy said. If she were going to delegate tasks to others, she also had to trust them.

Looking relieved, Poppy turned to her brother. "Reed, could your crew work a little quieter this weekend?"

"We're doing our best," he replied, brushing white wallboard dust from his thick, wavy hair. "Your timeline is aggressive. We'll move to the other side of the inn, though. I'll talk to them now."

"Thank you for doing that," Ivy called after Reed as he hurried away. She knew he would work as quickly as possible under the guidance of his father, Forrest. Ivy's brother managed larger construction projects, so Reed had grown up in the business.

They would have to make their remaining guests as comfortable as they could in what was rapidly becoming a major construction zone. However, they couldn't afford vacancies for long. That was why the inn would close during the most disruptive work. Reed promised his crew and other subcontractors would work as quickly as possible.

Even without guests, there was still plenty to do at the inn. Shelly would overhaul the grounds and prepare the garden, while Poppy would create the summer marketing campaign. Ivy would manage the budget and answer questions Reed needed resolved.

Ivy turned back to Poppy. "Who is our new guest?"

"Libby Connors." Poppy beamed. "She sounds very understanding. I don't think she'll pose a problem. And it's only for the weekend. I'll make sure to keep her out of harm's way."

What was another few days? Ivy knew what it was to be

without a place to stay. After her husband died suddenly, she'd sold their Boston condo she hadn't known was so highly mortgaged. She'd had difficulty finding another home. Having been a stay-at-home mother for years, she had little verifiable income aside from teaching part-time art classes.

Without cash deposits and a source of income, she couldn't rent an apartment. So when she discovered a room for rent in a professor's home, she had to take it for a few months until she could figure out her life. She had never felt so adrift. Her eldest daughter lived with roommates, and her youngest was traveling Europe for the summer.

Ivy pressed a finger to her temple as a flood of emotions filled her. Although it hadn't been easy, she had managed to transform her life. When she opened the inn, she had vowed not to turn away anyone who truly needed a place to stay.

Still, she was concerned about having guests now.

At least she didn't have to worry about Bennett, who was taking it all in stride. As the mayor of Summer Beach, he spent every day at his office. On the weekends, he kept busy with his boat or community events.

He'd done his share around the inn, helping keep it in good repair, even though it was Ivy's asset. Once, when she'd protested, he said, *If I can help make your life easier, why wouldn't I?*

He was definitely a keeper.

Shelly nudged her. "Are you okay?"

Ivy had to trust the process and her team. She swept a hand over her hair. "Sure."

"Then why do you have that look, Ives?"

Ivy was a little perturbed her sister could read her so well. "What look?"

"See? That look." Shelly grinned in triumph. "Like you forgot how fabulous this place will be when the work is complete. This is what we've needed. It's what you envisioned the first time you saw this old beast of a place. I still remember standing in the front yard when you had your epiphany about keeping the house and moving in. I was reluctant, but you knew what you wanted."

"It wasn't like we had any other place to go." Ivy chuckled at the memory. "Bennett was shocked, but we made it work for us."

"No thanks to him in the beginning," Shelly added, quirking a grin. "He thought he'd made a sale. Still, he turned out okay in the end. Bet you never thought he'd be your future husband."

"Not for a minute," Ivy said, slinging an arm around her sister. "I couldn't have done this without you. Or you, Poppy. You two are the marketing brains."

Their niece's delicate face flushed. "I love working here with you two." Poppy paused, frowning a little. "I'll sort of miss the old shabbiness, though. I hope it's not so fancy that guests are afraid to track sand from the beach inside."

"I want it to be comfortable," Ivy said. "Only with plumbing that works, lights that don't flicker, and windows that don't whistle in the wind."

Shelly laughed. "That's true luxury." Something outside caught her eye, and she peered from the window. "Chief Clarkson and Imani just pulled up."

"They're here to help Gilda move," Ivy said. "Since Jamir started medical school, Imani has extra room."

Jamir had helped her youngest daughter, Sunny, stay focused on her studies.

In the end, that had paid benefits. Sunny graduated and was awarded a scholarship for a master's program in hospitality. Now, she was away on a fieldwork assignment, consulting at a major hotel under her professor's tutelage.

A staccato clatter erupted on the stairs in the foyer.

"Pixie is loose," Shelly cried.

"I'll get her," Ivy said, racing to catch the Chihuahua before she escaped. Pixie and her guardian were relocating during the construction. "Would you direct Clark and Imani round the back to the car court?"

Ivy tried trapping Pixie on the last stairstep, but the dog broke through her clutch. Ivy gave chase.

Pixie round the corner and headed for the music room, leaping over electrical cords with nimble moves. She stopped in front of a wall, sniffed it, and began to bark.

Ivy swept her into her arms. "You almost made a break for it, didn't you? Silly dog, barking at walls." Cuddling the shivering little creature, she turned back to Shelly, who'd followed her.

Shelly frowned with concern. "Gilda and Pixie will return when the work is finished, won't they?"

"They're like family now," Ivy said, nodding. "Would you look out for Poppy's last guest? I need to return Pixie and see how Gilda is doing. She's feeling unsettled and displaced."

After Shelly agreed, Ivy climbed the stairs to Gilda's room.

Keeping a tight hold on Pixie, Ivy peered into the open door.

"Where in the world is your rhinestone collar?" Gilda muttered, rummaging through items strewn across the bed. Her bracelet, heavy with travel charms, jingled with every movement. "I swear I just had it in my hand."

Ivy suppressed her laughter. "If that belongs to Pixie, why don't you ask her yourself?"

"Good heavens, I thought she was right beside me. She wriggled out of her collar again."

"And she made a break for it. Likely for the beach." Ivy didn't want to concern Gilda with Pixie's strange behavior in the music room. "I think Pixie is jealous of Brother Rip's surfing collie." She handed the wayward pooch to Gilda and peered under the bed. "I see the collar way in the back. I can reach it for you."

"Pixie must have hidden it, didn't you, my sweetikins?" Gilda kissed Pixie's nose. "She's so anxious about the move. I need to schedule a therapy session for her."

Ivy scooted under the bed to retrieve the flashy dog collar. After returning it to Gilda, she surveyed the room, which still wasn't packed. "The chief and Imani just arrived. Do you need help to finish packing?"

"Oh, goodness. The time has slipped away, what with having to tend to Pixie, who doesn't understand what's happening." Gilda gave Ivy a look of gratitude. "A little help would be wonderful."

Ivy shut the door to keep Pixie inside and began to fold hoodies before placing them in an open suitcase on the bed. This guest room had been Gilda's home since the Ridgetop Fire in Summer Beach. It looked bare without her magazine article awards and travel photographs on the walls. Those and the knickknacks she'd collected filled boxes by the door.

Gilda put Pixie down and picked up her phone to make a call. "It's dead. Now, where did I put my charger?" She looked at every outlet, but didn't find it.

Ivy saw the tiny Chihuahua dart into the closet. "You might check in there."

"Pixie!" Gilda called her, and a few moments later, the Chihuahua emerged with a pink charging cord dangling from her mouth like a prize.

"Why, you little thief! Come to Mommy."

The dog pranced away, clearly enjoying the chase, then skittered under the bed and disappeared.

The door creaked open, and Imani looked inside. "Poppy sent me up. Anything ready to go into the pickup yet?"

Ivy shook her head. "Pixie has been up to her usual tricks." The little dog peeked out, looking guilty.

Imani laughed, her warm, throaty chuckle filling the room. "That sassy critter has more personality than most people I know."

"And better jewelry," Ivy added, joining in the laughter. "I'll bet she's stolen half the contents of this room."

A voice boomed behind Imani. "Do we have a thief on the premises?" Clark Clarkson, Summer Beach's Chief of Police and Imani's boyfriend, stood in the doorway, his broad shoulders nearly filling the frame.

"What can I take now?" he asked, eyeing the stack of half-packed boxes by the door.

Ivy transferred the thick hoodies into the boxes to fill them. "There. Two are ready to go. By the time you return, we'll have more."

"My hero," Imani said, a smile transforming her face. She squeezed his arm affectionately as he bent to hoist the boxes with ease.

"I didn't realize how much I'd accumulated," Gilda said. "How long has it been?"

"You moved in right after the fire with just two suitcases." Gilda lost her home in the fire and decided not to rebuild, saying life was easier and more comfortable here. "We'll have this done in no time."

Imani pitched in to help Ivy pack while Gilda emptied drawers. A few minutes later, a whimper drew their attention to the bathroom, where Pixie had created a nest of stolen items: dog toys, a silk scarf, and one of Gilda's slippers.

"Oh, sweetikins," Gilda cooed. "Mommy isn't leaving you. We'll have a beautiful new room with an ocean view at Auntie Imani's house."

Pixie gave her a skeptical look.

Ivy watched the interaction, a knot of worry forming in her chest. Despite the laughter, she was concerned about Gilda's adjustment. The slightly eccentric writer had become more than a guest; she was family.

And family looked out for one another. Ivy scooped up Pixie's ill-gotten gains and deposited them into a box.

Clark returned for more boxes, and Imani went with him, carrying the boxes she'd finished packing.

Once they were alone, Ivy continued packing. After a while, she turned to Gilda. "Are you concerned about being comfortable at Imani's? I know you like to write late into the night, and she's an early riser."

Gilda waved away her concern. "I've lived in dismal Parisian garrets and splendiferous Italian villas. I once scribbled a travel article from a Mongolian yurt, so I'll be fine in Imani's guest room." The corners of her mouth turned down. "It's Pixie who's worried."

Imani returned as Gilda was talking. "Jamir uses a white noise machine. He swears by it for studying and says it helped him through this first year of med school. I put a new one in your room to take the edge off unfamiliar background noises."

Ivy felt a rush of affection for her friend's thoughtfulness. "That sounds helpful."

Imani nodded at Gilda. "I also put a coffee maker in your room, so you don't have to emerge until you're fully caffeinated."

"Usually sometime after noon," Gilda said, smiling.

Ivy taped the last carton shut. "Sounds like Imani has thought of everything."

"Contingency planning is my superpower." Imani tucked a stray braided lock behind her ear, her expression softening. "Gilda will be fine. We'll have wine on the deck overlooking the ocean waves and watch the sunset. She can critique my wild wardrobe, and I'll pretend to understand her articles on traveling lightly."

Ivy laughed at the vision. "Hope I get an invitation soon."

These were her people. As different as they were from each other, they had formed a family of choice here in Summer Beach. The inn might be undergoing changes, but the relationships they'd built living together at the inn after the fire were solid.

Ivy walked Gilda to the door of her room. "I hope you'll return as our first guest when we reopen."

Gilda glanced back at the room with misty eyes. "I'm counting on it. This old beach house saved me after the fire. I was lost, everything gone. Until a new face in town welcomed us. You didn't ask questions when I showed up without a reservation."

Ivy hugged her. "And with a kleptomaniac Chihuahua. We've had our good times, and I promise we'll have many more when you return."

They went downstairs to the car court with the last of Gilda's belongings. Ivy watched Gilda and Imani get into the truck with Clark.

Poppy and Shelly joined her, waving as their longest-term guest left. "Feels like the end of an era."

"She'll be back," Shelly said. "Mom always said change is inevitable, but friendship is enduring."

"I sure miss Mom and Dad," Ivy said. "They'll be amazed at the transformation of this place." They were living their best retired life, sailing around the world together on a long-anticipated bucket trip.

As they watched Clark's pickup turn onto the street, another vehicle pulled in. It was a vividly painted recreational vehicle. "Could that be our new guest?"

"Probably," Poppy replied. "She asked if there was a place to park a larger vehicle."

Shelly let out a laugh. "Oh, my gosh. What the heck is that?"

The artist in Ivy appreciated the unusual paint job. She was even more curious about this new guest now.

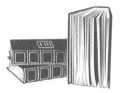

a younger woman wearing a long, flowing prairie-style dress with fancy cowboy boots swung out of the whimsically painted motorhome.

Shelly raised her brow. "Looks like an old, spruced up RV. So why isn't she sleeping in that?"

The young woman slung a backpack over her shoulder and started toward them.

Ivy waved to her. "Welcome to the Seabreeze Inn."

Introductions were made, and they led Libby through the rear door to the kitchen. Ivy decided to check her in there rather than guide her through the construction. She asked Poppy to get the tablet they used to register guests.

She gestured to a chair at the family table. "Would you care for a cup of tea while we check you in?"

"I'd love one, and thanks for accommodating me," Libby replied, taking in her surroundings with interest. "I hope I won't be too much trouble."

"We're happy to accommodate you," Ivy said. "We're

pretty casual now with the renovations under way." She poured a cup for Libby, and Poppy returned.

"Have you been camping in that?" Shelly nodded toward the unusual vehicle, curiosity lighting her face.

"There's very little room in there," Libby replied. "It's a bookmobile, so it's stuffed with books. I keep a small air mattress in there for emergencies, but it's not very comfortable."

Poppy's eyes glittered. "May we see inside?"

"Let's check in Libby and show her to her room first." Ivy smiled at her niece's enthusiasm. Poppy was an avid reader. They all were when they had the time.

"I'll be happy to take you on the mini tour later," Libby said, her cheeks coloring slightly. "It's a passion project."

Shelly tilted her head with curiosity. "How long have you been driving that?"

"About two years, coast to coast. I was laid off, so it was just for fun at first." Libby furrowed her brow. "Anyway, I'm on my way to Los Angeles to interview for a job, so I won't be taking her out much once I start working." With a wistful look, she gave a little shrug.

"What do you do?" Ivy asked, wondering about this young woman who would drive a bookmobile for fun.

Poppy's eyes were full of questions, too.

Libby's face brightened. "I'm a librarian. That is, I used to be. My position was eliminated during budget cuts. I thought this bookmobile adventure would be an escape for a couple of months. But I've been all over the country visiting communities that don't have a library nearby."

"How cool," Shelly said. "I'll bet you have a thousand stories."

Libby grinned shyly. "At least."

Poppy leaned across the table, lacing her fingers. "How do you decide where to go? Do people invite you, or is it something else?"

Libby studied her for a moment. "I like to think that I wind up where I'm needed to make a difference."

That was an interesting reply, Ivy thought, though she was used to visitors who expressed themselves in different ways. "Reading can certainly make a difference in people's lives, especially children."

"They're my favorite," Libby said. "Do you still have a library here?"

"We used to have a quaint little place." Ivy shook her head. "But a fire broke out in the restaurant next door. The library and most of the books were damaged. Very little could be salvaged."

"How sad," Libby said, her expression sympathetic. "I hope no harm came to the library staff or patrons."

Ivy appreciated the other woman's compassion. "It happened late at night, so no one was there. Our longtime librarian was heartbroken over the damage, so she retired. She's off traveling the world now."

Libby nestled her backpack beside her chair. "Are there plans to build another one?"

"Our community didn't have the budget to reopen the library," Ivy replied. "Despite my best efforts to lobby the mayor, nothing has changed. Everyone misses the library."

That remained a sore point between her and Bennett. Not that she didn't welcome book clubs, students, and story time for the little ones here, but Summer Beach lost an essential pillar of the community.

"What a shame," Libby said. "What can be done about it?"

"Nothing that a big chunk of funds wouldn't solve," Ivy replied.

Even as she spoke, a sense of loss filled her. Some of her fondest childhood memories were when her mother took her and her siblings to the library. They each had a library card with their name on it. That made Ivy feel grownup, so she kept hers safe.

"I miss it," Shelly said, the edges of her mouth drifting down. "My library card was a key to adventure. We could check out an armload of books. The library trusted us, and that meant a lot to me. Even though I had to work off a few books I lost in a rogue wave. Mom and Dad insisted on that."

"It was high tide, and you were too close anyway." Ivy laughed, recalling the day Shelly's books were swept out to sea.

Shelly made a face at Ivy. "The library was more than that. We had summer reading challenges, story times, and tutors. I studied there throughout school. The librarian showed me how to find books on plants and gardening, which stoked my interest in horticulture." She heaved a sigh. "It's a shame my daughter won't experience the joy of a community library."

With empathy etched on her face, Libby nodded. "People don't know what they've lost until it's gone."

"We try to help fill that void," Ivy said. "We host book clubs here at the inn on the lower level. Many of our retirees depended on the library for books and a sense of community."

While the inn had hosted the book clubs that met at Pages Bookshop after the earthquake, when the shop reopened, they all returned there. The recent library fire brought many more book clubs to the inn, as the library hosted several meetings each day.

Poppy spoke up. "Now several people share assigned books. They draw straws to see who reads it first, and I hear them arguing about how long their friends are taking."

Ivy smiled at Libby and gestured to Poppy's tablet. "I'm sure you've heard all this before, so we'll finish checking you in."

Poppy turned on the tablet. "Would you like to use a credit card for the room?"

Libby lowered her eyes and unzipped her backpack. "I'd rather pay by cash if that's okay. I can pay upfront."

"We're happy to accommodate you," Ivy said. She couldn't remember the last time someone paid cash for a room, but she had no problem with that. "I'll get my purse to make change for you."

"I'm sure I have it." Libby pulled a thick wad of crumpled bills in small denominations from her backpack.

Shelly's eyes widened. "Are you a stripper in your spare time?"

Ivy was mortified. "Shelly!"

"Not that there's anything wrong with that," Shelly added, raising her palms. "It's good exercise, right?"

Fortunately, Libby only laughed. "I sell a few books and take donations." She tapped her name on the digital guest register and counted out the exact change for the bill.

Poppy slid the money to Ivy and turned back to Libby. "Here's your key, and I'll show you to your room."

Libby hoisted her backpack. "Is it okay to leave the bookmobile there?"

"If you'll park it to one side so my husband can get into the garage, that will be fine."

Poppy stood. "I'll show you." She led Libby outside.

Ivy watched Libby start the vehicle and move it. "It's sad to think that Daisy won't be able to explore a local library until she goes to school." The next community down the coast had one, but it was on the farthest side of town from them and wasn't very convenient. They had scaled back on their hours and services due to budget cuts.

"I heard some schools are closing their libraries, too," Shelly said. "People think all kids are online, but the little ones like picture books. Daisy loves hers, even though she can't read. Still, she's learning her numbers from a book we read at bedtime."

"In Boston, I used to take Misty and Sunny to weekly story time at the library." Leaning against the center island, Ivy smiled at the memories. "That was before Jeremy made partner, so we were on a budget. I would bundle the girls against the cold, and we'd trudge through the snow. They had a chance for early socialization while I checked out books on parenting. That's where I made my first friends with other moms and their little ones. The library meant a lot to me; it helped me keep my sanity."

"I can imagine." Shelly put her hands on her hips. "You should talk to Bennett again about reopening the library. I don't think he tried hard enough to influence the city council last time. I still think he could pull a few strings and make it happen."

"It's not that easy." Ivy sighed. "There is no money in the city budget for a new library, and people don't want any new taxes. The city didn't own the property, the building was demolished, and the new buyer had other plans. So, the city lost out."

"I can't believe you've given up on this." Shelly put a hand on her hip. "We ought to do something about that."

"Now you want to help." Ivy winced. Did it look like she'd given up? "We've been over this before."

"But you're so good at making the impossible possible." Shelly waved a hand. "Just look at this place. You even made this renovation a reality."

"Technically, Viola did."

"And who tracked down Viola in San Francisco? And on an unscheduled layover during your honeymoon." Shelly bumped her fist. "Like I said, thanks to you. You've got that law of attraction mojo going for you."

Ivy laughed at the idea. "Maybe, but Shells, I can't make magic." *If only I could.* She shook her head. Though her desire to bring a library back to Summer Beach remained strong, life had served up an extra helping of challenges lately.

Her sister looked crestfallen. "You need to try again, Ives. If anyone can do it—"

"Not now." Still, what else could she do?

Shelly threw up her hands. "At least think about it. I'm sure you can come up with another plan."

"Then you do it," Ivy said. She was still grieving over the loss, and her sister wasn't making it any better. However, Shelly's eyes registered instant hurt. "Hey, I'm sorry. I didn't mean for it to come out that way."

Shelly quirked one side of her mouth in a lopsided grin. "We all believe in you. I'll help more this time. Daisy is sleeping through the night now, so I'm not such a zombie anymore."

"Please, Shelly. Just stop." Shaking her head, Ivy glanced at her watch. "I need to speak to Reed. He's somewhere outside."

"I saw him near the front."

Ivy hurried away. She was heartbroken over her inability to convince Bennett and the city council, but she understood. If there were no funds, that was that. At least as far as the city was concerned.

Wasn't it? She walked outside and strode across the lawn.

Besides, they were doing what they could to fill the void at the inn. They had promised the common spaces at the inn to anyone who wanted to use them as a substitute for the library.

Between scheduled weddings and other events, there was hardly a day that wasn't full of activities. Sometimes, it was almost too much, but she had made a promise.

Yet, Shelly's words touched a nerve. If she couldn't get approval from City Hall, maybe she could get the community behind the effort. It might take years to raise funds and gain approval, but it would be worth it.

Her husband would certainly have an opinion about that. Surely, they could agree that a library was good for the community.

Just then, her phone rang, and she answered. "Bennett, darling. I was just thinking of you."

His voice was as warm as sunshine. "Hope those were good thoughts, sweetheart."

"Always. I was thinking about the library again—"

"Ivy, we did all we could." Instantly, he sounded weary.

"Are you sure, though?" Ivy's grip on her phone tightened. Shelly's words of encouragement wouldn't mean anything to Bennett. Still, he was usually optimistic about Summer Beach projects. "We could go to the community—"

"Unfortunately, we have to let that idea go." He hesitated. "With so much chaos in the house, I thought we could avoid cooking tonight. I can grab tacos from Rosa's, and we can watch the sunset on the beach."

That was one of their regular romantic getaways. She didn't want to spoil it tonight. "That sounds perfect."

"I'm on my way."

She tapped her phone to disconnect. With a sigh, she realized Bennett had become as disillusioned over the library project as she was.

Still, she wondered if Shelly might be right. Was there a way to fund a library that wouldn't damage her marriage?

It seemed impossible, but as Shelly suggested, she decided that word shouldn't be in her vocabulary anymore.

Heartened by that thought, she straightened her shoulders. Maybe the third round of the Library vs. City Hall was about to begin.

4

*I*vy wound her way past the construction, stepping over electrical cords and avoiding the scaffolding for work on the second-floor windows and painting.

Her nephew was speaking to his crew while the men were packing tools.

"Hey, Reed, got a minute?"

"Sure. The guys will start work on the other side of the house." As his men left, Reed's phone interrupted with a song ringtone. After a quick glance, he frowned.

"Do you need to take that call?"

"I'm waiting to hear from a supplier, but this is something else." A look of dismay crossed his face as he shoved it into his pocket. "Or rather, it was. No surprise, though."

"Forrest told me you're dating someone." Reed was a smart, good-looking young man with a big heart. "Is that your girlfriend?"

"Not according to that text. She just broke up with me because I canceled our weekend plans. I don't like ultimatums, so I let her go."

Ivy was appalled. "She broke up in a text? Who does that?"

"No one I want to be with." Reed sighed. "It's more common than you think, Aunt Ivy."

"Maybe it's just a misunderstanding."

"She's a travel blogger, and she needs someone with free time to travel and film her." Flexing his jaw, he added, "That's not me. My work is here with Dad, and I love what I do. Someday, I want to build a home for my family in Summer Beach."

Ivy's heart went out to him. "Your dad was committed to work when he was starting the construction business. We always knew he would be successful."

"That's what it takes," Reed said, blowing out a breath. "At least you understand."

She paused, sizing up her nephew. He was tall and well-built from working in his father's construction business. More than that, Reed was a young man of substance and, judging from the sadness around his eyes, one who seemed ready for a partner. "Was it a serious relationship?"

Reed raised a hand and let it drop. "I thought so at first, but she clearly didn't share the big picture." He scuffed his work boot on the flagstone path. "Did you need to talk to me about the work?"

Ivy had almost forgotten. "I was looking at the plans this morning. Since we're making improvements, I wondered if we could create more storage in several places. I wanted to let you know before you got too far along. I have ideas, but I thought you might have a few, too."

"Sure. I'll look at the plans tonight and make notes."

Reed left to supervise his crew, leaving Ivy wondering how a young woman could let go of someone like him. Everyone had their priorities, she supposed. Maybe he didn't have scads of money to blow on expensive holidays, but he was smart and building a business under the tutelage of his father.

She liked to think he had a great family, too.

Just then, she saw the book club ladies arrive. She hurried to greet them.

Their neighbor Darla led the way, pushing a small baby stroller. The older woman's short, royal-blue hair and sparkly visor shone like a beacon in the sunlight.

Shelly met them in the entryway and reached for the little girl. "Hiya, sweetie. Did you have a good time with Granny Darla today?"

Daisy cooed her approval as Darla passed her to Shelly. "You bet she did. Daisy scoots on the floor faster than any child I've seen since my son was young. She's pulling up on the furniture, though she's still wobbly. Cute as a flower, she is." Darla tickled Daisy's neck, and the little girl laughed. She parked the stroller by the door.

Shelly kissed her child's fair curly hair. "Thanks for looking after her today. This place is such a mess. I was afraid she might get hurt."

"I'm happy to take care of her until this construction is over." Darla's gruff voice held a note of hope. "She'll be right next door anytime you want to check on her."

Relief filled Shelly's face. "That would be a huge help, at least for part of the day. We can work around Mitch's schedule, too. Once she starts walking, you might change your mind, though. With her energy, she'll be unstoppable."

"Like her mother," Darla said with a chuckle.

Ivy had never imagined Darla would look after Daisy like a grandmother. She'd been a grouchy neighbor when she and Shelly moved in. She even sued them. Thankfully, all that was in the past. Mitch had seen through Darla's gruff exterior and became the replacement for the son she'd lost years ago. With him came Shelly and now Daisy.

She'd never seen Darla look happier.

Jen from Nailed It hardware store stepped inside to greet them with hugs. "How are you doing with the construction?"

"It's progressing," Ivy said. "All guests will be gone by Monday, and everything will begin in earnest."

Jen surveyed the prep work, taking in the plastic-draped furnishings and the heavy paper on the wooden floor to protect it from damage. The vintage chandeliers would soon be removed for cleaning and rewiring. "Tell Reed we can make special deliveries as needed. That will save him time."

"I sure will," Ivy said.

Louise, a steel gray-haired woman who owned the laundry in the village, arrived next, clutching a book and a bottle of wine. "I just finished reading. What an incredible story."

More women and a few men arrived with their books, and chatter quickly rose in the air. This scene occurred a few times a week with different book clubs. Tonight was the sip-and-share club that read biographies and historical sagas. The romance readers club also met here, as did the men's club that liked thrillers, spies, and espionage.

Darla raised a hand and motioned everyone toward the lower-level staircase. "Let's go, I'm thirsty. Everyone downstairs."

With a few hoots from the crowd, they all clomped downstairs. This club meeting was the second today. This morning, the story time group had been here. Shelly had joined the parents with Daisy before Darla fetched her.

"That's a lively group today," Shelly said, bouncing Daisy on her hip.

Ivy grinned. "With those libations, they usually are." Providing space for community meetings was part of what Ivy had promised to raise funds for the historical restoration. Still, she enjoyed being part of the fabric of Summer Beach.

A few minutes later, construction sounds filled the air.

"Guess Reed's demolition crew relocated near us," Poppy shouted.

Ivy had to raise her voice, too. "Better than disturbing our paying guests."

"The book club won't like that," Poppy added.

They all looked at each other. Shelly raised her brow and began counting. "Ten, nine, eight, seven, six, five, four—"

Darla charged up the stairs. "What in heaven's name is that racket? We can't hear ourselves think, let alone discuss the book."

"I'm sorry, Darla, but we warned you," Ivy said, although she hadn't realized it would be quite so loud.

"I know, I know. But where can we go?"

Ivy blinked, trying to think of an option. Several club members often put up their extended family and friends at the inn, so they were important to keep happy, too.

"How about gathering around the fire pit on the beach? There are plenty of Adirondack chairs. It will be quieter out there, and it should be a beautiful sunset. We only have a couple of guests. They might even join you."

"Well, I suppose that will work," Darla said in a grudging tone. "Some people might have to take off their shoes." She looked down at her sneakers.

"Nothing like the feel of sand between your toes," Shelly said, giving Darla a high-five. "I'll even whip up some Sea Breeze cocktails for you."

Darla seemed to like that idea. Ivy flashed a grin at Shelly. "Take them through the kitchen and out the back door."

A few minutes later, the book club members were fleeing

the premises for the relative quiet of the beach, the sound of the waves crashing on the shore notwithstanding.

Poppy smiled, holding her hand over her ears. "That was quick thinking."

"Let's go to the kitchen," Ivy said. "Might be a little less volume back there."

However, before they could leave, the front door opened again. Two high school students and an older man stepped inside.

"David and Sophie," Ivy said, greeting them. "Are you here to study?"

"Yes, ma'am," Sophie replied. "Our midterm exams are this week, so we brought a tutor. I hope that's okay."

"It is, but it's pretty loud where you usually study."

Worried looks filled their faces. "I don't think we can study with that," David said.

Ivy felt sorry for these two siblings. They were the oldest in their house, and with several younger siblings, they had nowhere else to study. Usually, they sat quietly in the ballroom, out of the way. She knew how important their grades were to them. They were top students and hoped to gain scholarships to the university in San Diego or elsewhere.

Quickly, Ivy fished in her pocket for her key. "Take my apartment above the garage. You can study at the table. And help yourself to soft drinks and snacks in the refrigerator." Bennett wouldn't mind, and they wouldn't be home for a while anyway. She'd bring a bottle of his favorite wine.

Sophie looked relieved. "Thank you, but we always pack sandwiches."

"We're going that way now," Ivy said, motioning them to follow.

Ivy directed them through the kitchen, and as they crossed

the car court, she saw the book club members gathered around the bookmobile.

Curious, Ivy stepped into the car court, intrigued by the vintage RV-turned-bookmobile. Fantastical murals that warmed her artist's heart covered the exterior.

Darla gazed at the vehicle as if it were an answer to her prayers. "Would you look at this beauty?"

She looked closer. Towering castles sprouted from open books, dragons swooped through starlit skies, and mermaids dove through waves morphing into turning pages. The words *Adventures Await* splashed across the side in swooping calligraphy.

"Wow, that's breathtaking," Shelly said in awe, with Daisy wedged on her hip.

The little girl cried with glee, reaching toward the painted butterflies that seemed poised to flutter away. Shelly kissed Daisy's cheek. "This is like something from a fairytale. And not one of those scary warning fairytales, but the happy kind we read, right, Daisy-do?"

Darla circled the RV, her bedazzled visor catching the sunlight. "This is what Summer Beach needs."

A thought struck Ivy, but before she could speak, Darla's face filled with excitement.

"This is for Summer Beach, isn't it?" Darla clasped her hands. "I knew you and Bennett would work out something for us."

"Why, it must be." Louise's face lit. "I can hardly wait to tell everyone. Will it open tomorrow?"

Ivy's heart fell at their excitement. "It's really not—"

"I can open it." Libby emerged from the driver's side, smiling. "I'm an itinerant librarian. Tomorrow, I can park somewhere in Summer Beach and open for checkouts. You can follow me on social media to see where I'm stopping and when I'll return."

"So you're just passing through?" Louise's elated expression faded. "Couldn't you stay a while? We haven't had a library since the fire, and the children will be thrilled."

Ivy touched Louise's shoulder. "Libby's our guest. She just checked in for the weekend."

Libby's face flushed. "I could stay a little longer if people would like to check out books."

Although everyone would like that, Ivy didn't want to trouble their guest or cause a construction delay. "Don't you have a job interview in Los Angeles?"

Libby pressed her lips together for a moment. "I could probably reschedule it."

"We couldn't let you risk that position." Ivy shook her head. "As I explained, the construction level will escalate next week. We must close to guests due to liability concerns."

"Oh, sure," Libby said quickly. "I understand. I could return to Summer Beach in a couple of weeks. On the weekend, I mean. If I get the job."

Something in Libby's voice struck Ivy as odd, but their guest's business was none of hers.

Shelly stepped closer to admire the vehicle. "I've never seen anything like this. Those colors are extraordinary. That ocean blue there, it's practically luminous."

"Whoever painted this is incredibly talented." Ivy had an idea. "I have a friend whose business is food trucks. There aren't many people who work at this level of quality. I'm sure she'd love to see this so she could recommend your person to others."

"It was just someone I knew back home." Libby seemed a little nervous. "I think they moved away."

"Maybe they have a website?"

"I don't think so."

Ivy noticed the way Libby's fingers twisted together, and the slight tension in her shoulders. There was a story there, but clearly not one their guest wanted to share.

"Well, it's magnificent," Ivy said, steering the conversation. "How many books do you carry onboard?"

Libby's posture relaxed slightly. "I've never counted. The books come and go. I take donations of new titles, and when I have too many, I sell a few. I try to have something for everyone. Children's books, bestsellers, classics. Even large print editions."

"Sure wish you could stay a while," Darla said, looking disappointed. "When Mayor Bennett sees this, maybe he could work out something for the community."

Libby's eyes flashed at the perceived opportunity. "I'd be open to that, as long as it paid what the job in Los Angeles does."

Ivy sent Darla a warning glance, though she understood the other woman's impulse.

Darla edged closer and touched her shoulder. "Maybe you could talk Bennett into it."

"Just because we're married doesn't mean I have influence over his city business." Many people in town assumed that. Bennett made the separation clear, and Ivy respected that. Although admittedly, she had overstepped the boundary on the library. "Besides, we can't hijack Libby's personal vehicle."

Libby adjusted her backpack. "In the meantime, where could I set up tomorrow?"

"You should park by Java Beach," Darla offered. "I'll talk to the owner about it. He's like my son."

Shelly brightened at the suggestion. "Books and coffee. Mitch would like that."

"You might need city approval to park there," Ivy said.

Knowing how Bennett felt about this, she didn't want to take any chances. She'd mention it to him. Maybe not tonight, though. Early in the morning should give them enough time, and he was always in a good mood after a morning run that flooded him with feel-good endorphins, or whatever they were.

"Really, Ives. Who would she be hurting?" Shelly stepped closer to the RV, pointing out a detail to Daisy. "Look at the little reading mice in the corner there."

The tension broke as everyone gathered to spot the whimsical details hidden throughout the mural. Ivy watched as Libby relaxed, answering questions about her favorite books and the challenges of driving such a large vehicle.

Still, she saw something in the young woman's eyes. Wariness, perhaps, or sadness. She sensed the cheerful artwork might be concealing more than books.

Libby opened the rear door. "The inside is even better. Would you like to see it?"

Though the book club members were eager to look inside, Ivy hesitated, rubbing a tickle on her neck. The story of Pandora's box sprang to mind. She blinked to dispel it.

"Come on, Ivy." Shelly stepped inside. "Oh, my gosh. You need to see this. And I have to call Mitch. Be right back."

Shelly wedged past her with Daisy, and Ivy wondered if Bennett was on his way. She glanced behind her. Not seeing him, she stepped into the bookmobile.

Instantly, she felt transported to a magical world.

5

G lad to have left City Hall and the challenges of the day behind him, Bennett ducked through the back entrance of Java Beach, the screen door slamming shut behind him. The coffee shop was closed, but Mitch often stayed to clean up and make dinner to take home to Shelly and Daisy.

Late afternoon sunlight filled the small kitchen, illuminating the stainless-steel surfaces.

Jerry Garcia's voice floated over the clatter in the kitchen, with Mitch singing along as he worked.

Bennett chuckled. Once a Grateful Dead fan, always a fan. "Hey, where's the party?"

Mitch spun around, spoon in hand, his spiky sun-bleached hair matching his attitude. "Right here, man." He was in his element here, wearing faded jeans, worn kitchen clogs, and a vintage T-shirt that read, *Life's a beach and then you surf.*

With a grin, Mitch turned down the music and crossed the kitchen for a quick bro hug. "Almost ready. I threw together tacos, burritos, and nachos. Everyone likes Mexican take-out night."

Bennett breathed in deeply, savoring the aromas. "Smells great. Before you called, I planned to pick up tacos from Rosa's and take Ivy to the beach for the sunset."

"Change of plans, dude. That's how Shelly and Ivy roll." Mitch returned to the stove, stirring a green tomatillo sauce. He nodded to himself and turned off the burner.

"Do you know why?" Bennett had tried to call Ivy, but she didn't pick up. Maybe she'd forgotten to turn on the ringer.

Mitch shrugged as he worked. "Shelly said there's something we need to see at the inn, and I should bring you and dinner for everyone."

Bennett leaned against the counter, snagging a slice of avocado from the prep area. "Any idea what this is about?"

"Nope. She was being mysterious. Guess she wants it to be a surprise." Mitch ladled the tomatillo sauce into a container before turning to prep the tacos with rapid precision.

"That means they're up to something." Bennett watched Mitch add shredded cabbage, tomatoes, and sliced avocado. He garnished each with leafy cilantro and a wedge of lime. "Need help?"

"Sure, wash your hands and wrap these to go."

Bennett moved to the sink. "Maybe it's about the house. Reed might have found an issue. Though it was well built, that house is more than a hundred years old."

Mitch shook his head. "Shelly wouldn't sound excited about that. She was practically vibrating through the phone. Said we had to see something before tomorrow morning."

BEHIND MITCH, old surf competition photos lined the kitchen's back wall. The rest of Java Beach carried the same relaxed

Polynesian vibe with vintage travel posters, nautical nets, and tiki torches.

After washing his hands, Bennett began to wrap the tacos and pack them in to-go containers lined up on the counter.

Mitch quickly folded flour tortillas with refried beans and shredded cheese into burritos. "I want to see what Reed's been doing at the house anyway. Shelly wants a gardening shed, and I need my garage back. Maybe I'll pick up a few building tips."

Bennett grinned. "Because Daisy's room addition worked out so well last time?"

"Hey, I have vision," Mitch said, his eyes crinkling as he laughed.

"Is that what you call it? I seem to remember an unfortunate incident with a hammer, among other things."

"I call that architectural innovation, my friend." Mitch's grin was infectious. "So I like to live vicariously through Reed's competence."

"Guess I'm building Shelly a shed next." Bennett shook his head, but he enjoyed Mitch's company. He'd call some friends, and they'd have it done in a weekend. Mitch would gladly feed them all for that. He was industrious and always treated his friends in exchange for favors.

Most folks who lived in Summer Beach were like that. But it was more than that. He and Mitch had a long history. Long before Ivy and Shelly arrived in town, eager to sell the old house Ivy's late husband had bought, unbeknownst to her.

Mitch might have been sleeping in his car after he was released from a year in prison for a teenaged mistake, but it was his optimism and hustle, selling coffee on the beach to sunrise surfers, that inspired Bennett to help him. Darla stepped in, too, and they helped Mitch get the funds he needed to open Java Beach.

Today, it was one of the most popular spots in town.

As he loaded the food into insulated bags, Bennett wondered why Shelly had called, not Ivy. "What do you think they're up to?"

Mitch shrugged, finishing the nachos. "With those two? Could be anything. Nothing would surprise me anymore." He wiped down the counters and tossed a towel into a basket.

Bennett picked up the food. "Let's see what's going on."

6

"Come on in," Libby called out, flicking on the bookmobile's interior lights. "There's room for everyone. It's larger on the inside, like the Tardis."

Ivy laughed at the *Dr. Who* reference and stepped inside, following Darla, Jen, Louise, and other book club members. Exclamations of delight quickly filled the air. Immediately, Ivy was struck by how the interior seemed larger than possible.

Somebody had thoughtfully utilized the space, yet nothing felt cramped. Wooden shelves lined the walls, their warm honey color showcasing a rainbow of book spines. Clever brass library lamps were mounted between sections, casting a warm glow that made the space feel cozy rather than confined.

Shelly hurried back into the bookmobile with Daisy. "What did I miss?"

Ivy gestured toward a donation box and a shelf for books for sale. "That's why Libby had the exact change for her room," she whispered. "This is how she makes her living."

"She's pretty creative," Shelly said, bouncing Daisy on her hip. "A privately owned bookmobile. Who would've thought?"

Now in her element, Libby transformed. She grew more animated and confident as she showed off carefully organized, hand-painted shelves and a reading nook stuffed with lounge pillows in the form of animals.

"She's good with people," Shelly murmured.

"And she knows her books," Ivy added. "She has a nice assortment of the latest beach reads, biographies, children's picture books, and gardening guides. She knows her patrons."

Shelly leaned in. "Wish we could keep her here in Summer Beach. Are you sure there's no way we could?"

Ivy shook her head. "If she gets that job in Los Angeles, she won't be far. Maybe she'll visit again if she's not too busy."

In the reading nook, Louise plopped onto a plush purple turtle and howled with laughter when she couldn't get up. Darla tried pulling her to her feet but stumbled on a stuffed elephant and crashed beside her.

Laughing, Libby stepped in to help them both to their feet, and Shelly gave her a hand.

"No worries, this happens a lot," Libby said, smiling.

Once on her feet again, Darla and Louise thanked them and headed toward the sale rack.

Libby turned to Ivy and Shelly. "Did you see the ceiling?"

Ivy tilted her head back to take in more whimsical paintings. Someone painted the entire length to resemble library endpapers, with swirling marbled patterns in deep shades of scarlet, gold, and ocean blue. Author quotes rendered in calligraphy wove around the perimeter. One in particular caught her eye.

Literature is my Utopia. – Helen Keller

"The quotes glow in the dark," Libby said, noticing Ivy's interest. "A little paint magic that enchants children when I dim the lights."

"Did the same artist who painted the outside do this?" Shelly asked.

Libby nodded as she ran her hand along the smooth wood. "The shelves are custom built. They're angled just enough to keep the books secure while driving, and each section has a bar that pulls across the front for extra security."

Ivy was enchanted. "What a magical setting you've created. You seem to have thought of everything." She touched a narrow retaining bar across a bookshelf. "Our parents have something like this on their boat."

"Those are critical for rough seas and rocky roads," Libby said.

"Your books are so well organized." Ivy took note of the thoughtful, meticulous displays. She opened one, noticing the old-fashioned style pocket on the inside. The borrowing card featured a line of numbers and date stamps.

"Not all the books make it back, but I also get a lot of donations, so it all works out."

Children's picture books occupied lower shelves so little ones could reach them. Young adult novels had their own section marked with fanciful hand-painted signage. Fiction was arranged by genre, with small painted plaques marking different sections: mysteries, romance, thrillers, and science fiction.

Ivy noticed numbers on the spine, just like a real library. The Dewey Decimal System, she recalled.

"Old habits die hard," Libby said. "I try to maintain my standards."

"How can you leave this charmed life behind?" Shelly asked.

"It's time I had a real job with benefits and contributed to a community." Libby's voice held a note of wistfulness. "I like making new friends but miss seeing familiar faces."

"I understand." Ivy felt like that when she moved away from home. She'd been a homesick student. Maybe that's why she'd fallen so hard for Jeremy. Eventually, Boston became home to her, but it had taken time.

Across from them, Darla scooped up an armload of paperbacks and deposited cash into an antique wooden lunch pail. The vintage piece was marked *Honor Bar* and painted with a stack of books and an icy drink with a lemon slice. An umbrella tilted above it.

Ivy squinted at the scene. "Looks like lemonade."

"I was imagining a Long Island iced tea," Shelly said. "Chill, swill, and read your fill."

Libby gestured to an inviting chair near a window. "My favorite spot for that is right there. Sometimes, I park near a beach and read for hours."

"I can see why," Ivy said. "You've created a rolling oasis." She wanted to tell Paige, who owned Summer Beach's only bookshop, Pages Books, about this. She would love it.

"Look at this," Louise called out, opening a narrow door featuring a steaming mug. "A coffee station."

The small kitchen held a small under-cabinet refrigerator, an electric kettle, and a coffee maker. Tins of coffee, tea, nuts, and biscotti lined the small shelf above the counter.

"I often host book club teas," Libby said. "Or under a canopy I carry in the luggage compartment. Readers like special events."

At once, Daisy squealed, pointing to a basket of bright fabric books in the children's section.

"Those are special," Libby said. "Handmade for the youngest readers. Would she like to look at one?"

While Shelly helped Daisy explore the fabric books festooned with bright yarn and buttons, Ivy took in more details. A bookmark exchange, handwritten recommendation cards tucked into books, a printed card that read *Libby's Book-mobile*. Children's drawings and notes of appreciation posted to a corkboard. Ivy stepped closer to read them.

I didn't like reading until the bookmobile came to town. Now I love it. Come back soon. We love you, Libby!

The younger woman clearly loved books and knew how to make others love reading, too. How Ivy wished they had a library like this in town.

She turned to Libby. "You're so talented and well organized. You've created such a sweet retreat here."

"That's what I wanted it to be." Libby smiled, averting her eyes. "A place where anyone could find an adventure or a safe space."

Ivy detected conflicting emotions in Libby's face. Pride in what she'd accomplished yet edged with something unsettling.

Ivy wondered what she was concealing.

As an innkeeper, her job was to welcome visitors, give them shelter and kindness, and see them on their way. Still, some people shared their secrets, confiding in her because she was a kind stranger. They would return to their lives refreshed, their burden lightened, trusting Ivy wouldn't share their confessions with anyone they knew.

Libby raised her gaze to Ivy with a timid expression. "Could we talk while I'm here? About the history of the inn," she added quickly. "I'm curious about it."

Ivy recognized that look. "I'll be here."

Shelly glanced from the window and scooped up Daisy in her arms. "We should go. Mitch and Bennett are here. They brought dinner for us."

"Bennett and I have other plans," Ivy said. She had been looking forward to relaxing with him tonight.

"Not anymore," Shelly said. "I made the call. He's bringing a feast, and we can eat by the pool. Reed can join us and—" Shelly swung around. "Libby, do you like Mexican food? We have plenty."

"I'd like that, thank you." A smile lit Libby's face.

"And let's show them the bookmobile," Shelly added. "We'll be right back."

As they disembarked, Ivy turned to Shelly. "What are you up to?"

"Who, me?"

Her sister feigned innocence, but Ivy wasn't falling for it. "You want Bennett to see what the town is missing."

"I'm not responsible for any conclusions someone might draw," Shelly said. "I only wanted to ask Mitch if Libby could park in front of Java Beach tomorrow."

"You're lying." Ivy shook her head. "And it's brilliant," she whispered.

Hearing a commotion, Ivy turned to see Bennett and Mitch approaching from the car court, laden with carryout bags from Java Beach.

Her heart still quickened at the sight of her husband. She smiled and waved to him.

"Dinner has arrived," Bennett called out, hoisting the bags. "Tacos, nachos, and burritos with all the fixings." He greeted Ivy with a kiss. "Let's have our private sunset supper tomorrow."

"I'd like that," she replied. "Perfect timing for dinner. The book club is relocating to the firepit for their meeting."

Bennett's gaze drifted behind her, catching sight of the new vehicle. "What did you and Shelly want us to see?"

Ivy gestured over her shoulder. "Our new guest is a librarian. She arrived in her bookmobile. It's so charming and well-organized."

"Is it now?" Bennett took it in but made no other comment.

"Hope you're all hungry," Mitch said, kissing Daisy's cheek.

"Utterly starved." Shelly hugged Mitch. "The bookmobile is fabulous inside, babe. You guys should see it before we eat. Libby can park it in front of Java Beach in the morning. That paint job alone will draw people right to your front door."

Darla waved and greeted Bennett. "Glad you're here, Mr. Mayor. This bookmobile is incredible. If Summer Beach can't afford a library, how about one of these?"

"Is this an ambush?" Bennett asked with a slight frown.

"Not at all," Darla replied. "Just a happy accident. But you ought to go inside. The community would love something like this."

"It's even more amazing inside," Louise added, her eyes flashing with excitement. "Although we all miss having a library, this is a lot better than nothing."

Bennett raised his brow at Ivy. "I thought we'd laid that proposal to rest."

"This was a surprise to me, too," Ivy said, noting his discomfort. Changing the subject, she added, "We can put some tables together and eat by the pool. How much food did you bring?"

"Plenty," Bennett said, his frown relaxing. "Maybe Reed would like to join us."

Ivy heard Shelly introducing Libby to Mitch, who promptly invited her to join them for dinner, too.

"Would you like to see inside?" Libby asked.

"This is so cool," Mitch said. "What a paint job. Come on, Mr. Mayor. Let's take the tour."

Ivy and Poppy took the food from the guys so they could tour the vehicle with Libby.

"I can manage setting up the tables," Ivy said to Poppy. "Why don't you find Reed? He's probably hungry."

"He'll appreciate this," Poppy said, leaving to find her brother.

Ivy dusted off the tables and chairs and put the take-out bags in the center. The book club group started toward the beach with their books and wine bottles, though Darla hung back.

She paused by the table, her face drawn with worry. "I hope I didn't upset Bennett with what I said. It's just that a bookmobile would be a good compromise."

Ivy touched her hand. "It's not you, Darla. I don't know if the city can handle additional expenses this year. The state and federal funds that would normally be available aren't due to budget reductions. He feels bad because he knows how much residents want to replace the library."

Darla nodded. "You're so good at figuring things out. I thought you could persuade him."

"It's not a matter of that," Ivy said. "It comes down to finances. If I had a magic wand, I'd conjure a fabulous library for Summer Beach, but I'm fresh out of spells this time."

Darla hugged her. "Until then, we appreciate you letting us invade your space here at the inn. And we'll keep working on that new library."

"I love your optimism," Ivy said, smiling at her neighbor. She went inside to the kitchen to assemble serving utensils, paper plates and napkins, and cups and beverages for dinner.

Bennett and Mitch emerged from the bookmobile as she set the table.

"Perfect timing," Ivy said, looking up to see Poppy and Reed walking toward them.

"Thanks for the invitation," Reed said. "I worked through lunch and hardly had time to take breaks. I can't stay long."

Ivy knew how committed Reed was to the job. "I'm glad you joined us. You're family. Feel free to raid the kitchen anytime. We can't have our contractor starving."

"That's nice of you to say, but Dad's the contractor. I'm supervising." Reed looked up at the bookmobile in awe, then did a subtle double-take as Libby emerged. Their eyes met briefly, and Libby offered a bashful smile before quickly looking away.

"Join us, Libby," Ivy offered. "I'd also like you to meet our construction supervisor, who is also my nephew."

"Maybe I should get some work done." Libby hesitated, but Ivy could see the hunger in her eyes.

"At least take a plate with you. Mitch is quite the chef. Did you work out something for tomorrow?"

"Sure did," Mitch said. "I've never seen anything like that bookmobile. She can park it there for a week for all I care. People will love seeing it."

"And checking out books, I hope," Libby added with a small smile.

Ivy didn't want to ask Bennett what he thought of Libby's project, but she didn't have to. The awe in his face said it all; he was intrigued. He'd talk about it when he was ready.

Noticing Reed and Libby sneaking glances at each other, Ivy introduced them. "Reed, Libby is here with us for the weekend before she continues to Los Angeles."

Libby gave him a shy smile. "Reed. What a great name. And do you?"

"Sorry," he replied, slightly confused. "Do I what?"

"Read, as in books," Libby replied. "I hope you do."

The tips of Reed's ears turned pink. "Sure, when I can. I mostly read about construction. I'm studying for my general contractor's license. Does that count, or only novels?"

"Nonfiction is reading, too," Libby said. "I also count

audiobooks, even though there's debate about that. Anytime we're enriching our mind, it's a good thing."

"I liked reading Hemingway and Steinbeck in school," Reed said, pulling a chair at the table out for her.

"I would have guessed that about you." She suggested a couple of other authors he might like.

They sat beside each other, and Ivy watched their exchange with interest.

"Well, would you look at that instant attraction," Shelly whispered. "Interesting."

"Shh," Ivy said. "Libby isn't here long, and Reed is on the rebound. Don't get any ideas."

"It's not as if L.A. is in another country."

Ivy wagged a finger. "Don't try to fix them up."

"Doesn't look like they need any help."

"Don't you have to feed Daisy?"

Shelly shrugged. "I've been weaning her, and Poppy has her now." Shelly nodded to their niece.

Poppy walked Daisy around the patio, holding the toddler's hands as the little girl practiced steps. She grinned at them. "Look who's trying to walk."

Mitch stopped in front of them and opened his arms to her. "Come to Daddy, Daisy-cakes."

Suddenly, Daisy flung her hands free. Everyone froze as she wobbled, then took a determined step toward Mitch. Then another, and another. Mitch crouched down, arms outstretched, beaming with joy and encouragement as their daughter took her first steps straight to her papa.

She took four steps before she stumbled. Mitch swooped her into his arms as she fell. "That's my girl," he said, smothering her with kisses.

"She's walking," Shelly burst out, tears springing to her eyes. She rushed to hug Daisy, too.

Everyone erupted in cheers and applause as Mitch spun Daisy around while she giggled. "That's our girl."

Ivy laughed, thrilled for them. "Everything changes now. Better move all the breakables at your home right away. There's no going back."

Everyone settled around the patio table, and Mitch brought out the food, passing containers of tacos, nachos, and burritos. There were more with limes, cabbage, tomatoes, tortilla chips, and guacamole.

"This one is for Daisy," Mitch said, handing Shelly a container with avocado, diced banana, and other soft foods he'd prepared.

With the sun setting over the ocean, Ivy squeezed Bennett's hand and gazed around the table. "It's a beautiful sunset, after all."

The sound of construction seemed distant here, masked by the ocean breeze and the happy chatter of family.

"The crew's making good progress," Reed said between bites. "We should finish the electrical work in the music room tomorrow."

Ivy spoke up. "You mentioned we could still make changes at this stage."

"I'm sure we can create the storage you want," he replied, nodding.

She glanced at Bennett, wondering what he'd think about this. But the property belonged to her, so this was her decision. "Let's talk about it tomorrow. I appreciate all the work you're doing."

Ivy's mind was already racing ahead to the next phase. The timeline was tight, and there were so many details to tend to. They also had to pack and move items from one room to another to avoid damage.

As if reading her mind, Bennett reached for her hand. "I'll help you in the morning. We'll manage, sweetheart."

The conversation turned to Libby and her travels in the bookmobile. She had remarkable experiences to share. She told them how she crisscrossed the country, visiting northern states in summer and going to warmer southern states in winter.

As Libby spoke, Ivy sensed she was telling a story. She blinked, trying to dispel that strange thought. People often glossed over difficulties they'd had.

Ivy figured Libby's travels weren't all rosy and picture-perfect, but why spoil a good story? Everyone was enjoying the conversation.

"And where are you from originally?" Shelley asked.

"Oh, here and there." Libby hesitated. "My family moved around a lot."

Poppy leaned in. "And where did you study to be a librarian?"

Another hesitation. "That's a long story for another day."

"I hope to see you around," Reed said, quickly rising.

"I'll be busy with the bookmobile tomorrow, but I enjoyed meeting you. Good night, everyone." Libby hurried toward her room.

Shelly turned to Ivy with a questioning look. "Was that odd?"

Ivy thought so, too, but she lowered her voice. "Remember, guest business is none of our business."

7

That evening after Ivy changed and slid into bed, Bennett wrapped his arms around her. "That was nice of you to give the rest of the food to Sophie and David. And to suggest they study here."

"I'm glad you didn't mind. They needed a quiet space with their tutor. The scholarships they need to apply for will depend on good grades."

"Sweetheart, I admire what you do for the community and the passion you have for projects. But I worry about you becoming overextended and passing up paid guest events because of community commitments here. Be careful that you don't overdo your service to folks. You're still running a business."

"That only happened once. Maybe twice, but everyone understood. We made alternate arrangements." Ivy couldn't help adding, "I was thinking about the library situation—"

Bennett's jaw tightened almost imperceptibly. "We've been over this."

"I know, but with the bookmobile here, it reminds me how much the community needs—"

Bennett cut in, his tone gentle but firm. "We can't change that, even for a good cause."

Ivy tried again. "We talked about a fundraiser, like the gala we gave for Viola."

"You were the only one willing to do it." With a sigh, he took her hand. "This renovation has turned out to be more time consuming than intended. Reed and his crews are all working overtime. There are only so many hours in the day, even for you."

"As I watched Daisy starting to walk, I thought about her and all the children in Summer Beach who will grow up without a library to explore. What if the city made an offer to Libby to stay and provide her bookmobile as city service."

Bennett ran a hand over his jaw. "That's an interesting idea, but—"

"No money, right?" Ivy sighed.

"I was going to say she'd need to submit a proposal. We don't know anything about her or her work beyond what we saw today. I liked her, but she seemed evasive at dinner."

"You picked up on that, too?"

"I could feel the vibes you were giving off." He drew a hand over her hair. "I've found that when I push too hard on projects fraught with challenges, it might not be the right time for it. I worry you'll overextend yourself, that's all."

"And yet, you've always said you're proud of my resourcefulness."

Bennett hesitated before nodding. "Okay, point taken. Just know the city budget has its limitations."

"Good thing I'm resourceful, then."

"This is one more reason I love you," Bennett said, grinning.

"I hope you never run out of reasons," she said, kissing him softly. "Because I sure won't."

She loved that they could talk about their concerns now. They'd had to work on that when they first married.

"I'll talk to Libby over breakfast," she said. "If not her, maybe there's another solution." There had to be one; she just hadn't found it yet.

On the other hand, her husband had a point. She had pushed so hard on the library project. In the end, it didn't seem like it was meant to be. Maybe having an occasional visit from a traveling bookmobile was the best solution.

For now.

Ivy thought about the community's limitations and Bennett's concern for her. Still, she was passionate about filling this need for Summer Beach residents at some point.

WITH ONLY TWO guests in the dining room for breakfast, Ivy gave them extra attention. She chatted with Dr. Kempner, who shared a story from her service as a physician in the Navy.

"I remember it like it was yesterday," Meryl said, her eyes suddenly misting. "Some of my former colleagues are organizing a reunion now." Dabbing at the corner of her eyes, she sniffed back emotion. "Sorry, we lost one of us. He was always trying to get us together, but what with families and our minor aches and pains, we never quite managed. None of us knew he was ill. We were too late for him."

"But not for each other," Ivy said.

Meryl nodded with a wistful smile. "We're mostly retired now, so we plan to meet more often."

"You're young to be retired." Meryl didn't seem but a few years older. Ivy couldn't imagine not having the to-do lists she lived by every day. "How do you fill your time?"

"I do a lot of volunteering. I'm planning to start a charity for kids and teenagers who need guidance or a hand up."

"That's a wonderful idea."

Meryl told her she would be leaving later in the day, and Ivy told her how much she had enjoyed having her. They chatted a little more until Ivy excused herself to check on Libby.

Ivy held a coffee pot aloft. "Would you like a refill on your coffee?"

Libby looked up from her book and nodded. Looking contemplative, she asked, "All the work you're doing here must be costing a fortune."

"I'm afraid it is."

"How are you managing to pay for it all?"

"We're making do."

"How, exactly?"

Ivy was a little taken aback at that. "We're resourceful."

"I don't mean to pry," Libby said quickly, backing off her inquisitiveness. "I'm curious by nature, so I always wonder how entrepreneurs manage to do what they do."

"Is that your goal someday?"

"Sort of. Did you take out a loan or stumble into a huge inheritance?"

"Neither." Ivy relaxed a little into the conversation. Libby seemed socially awkward, so maybe she meant no harm. "We raised money for the work. This property is important to the community."

A thoughtful look filled Libby's face. "I imagine this place has a lot of history."

"It sure does."

Resting her chin in her hand, Libby seemed to choose her words with a certain nonchalance. "I've heard about Amelia Erickson."

Ivy wasn't surprised. "She was a fascinating woman who stood up for what she believed in. We hosted a gala fundraiser here to preserve the historical importance of her work."

Libby's face brightened. "Now that you mention it, I think I saw some photos from the event."

Ivy nodded at that. The inn and the fundraising gala that Viola had helped organize had received widespread press. Photos from the event were shared all over the internet.

Thankfully, she hadn't worn that fluffy pink prom dress she'd hastily picked up at the thrift shop; that grave lapse of judgment would have been immortalized on social media. Her mother and Bennett had surprised her with an elegant, understated outfit perfect for the occasion.

Libby leaned forward with a conspiratorial look. "I heard the Ericksons earmarked money for other buildings in Summer Beach."

That was news to Ivy. "I don't know anything about that."

"Since you bought the house from the estate, were you curious to see if she left other properties or projects in her estate?"

Ivy shifted on her feet. "My late husband bought the house. I didn't know about it until after he died. I don't talk about that much."

Libby looked surprised. "Oh. Do you know where the rest of her wealth went?"

Ivy was growing uncomfortable with the conversation centered on money. "As I understand, everything went to charity."

"But what about that necklace you sold and the other jewelry and art you've found? Have you looked for anything else?"

Ivy had heard these questions before from other modern day treasure hunters. She needed to set Libby straight in case she was entertaining the idea. "Most of the items we found belonged to other people. We've been over every spot in this house, especially with the renovation underway. I assure you, there is nothing else. I hope that's not why you're here."

Libby's cheeks reddened, and she mumbled an apology. "I've heard some rumors, that's all."

"Don't believe everything you hear," Ivy said. "Now, if you'll excuse me, I have to tend to something."

Ivy hurried to the kitchen, where she saw her niece. "I thought you would sleep in."

"Good morning," Poppy said. "Turns out I couldn't sleep very late. Do we have any of that homemade yogurt left?"

"In the fridge." Seeing Poppy reach for one of the twin turquoise refrigerators, she added, "The yogurt is in Bertie, not Bert. I'll have one, too."

Poppy opened the door and pulled out two small cups of yogurt. "Do you plan to replace these vintage beauties with sleek stainless-steel models?"

"I thought about it, but the commercial size we'd need would be expensive. As long as these units are working, we could use those funds for something else. What do you think?"

"I think you're right." Poppy handed her a yogurt. "I'd miss these. They're so cute."

"Then I'll have them serviced." She sat on a stool across from Poppy at the long kitchen island. They stirred honey and cinnamon into the tart yogurt.

She hadn't planned many renovations to the kitchen or their quarters other than necessary updates to electrical, plumbing, and other systems. The large kitchen was likely designed for the Erickson's frequent entertaining, so it was suitable for their purposes, too. After Bennett surprised her with a dishwasher, there wasn't much else she needed, other than additional electrical outlets and updated fixtures for the sink.

She would save money where she could in case there were unforeseen overages.

If there was enough left over, she planned to service the ovens and regrout the tile. She liked the house the way it was, except for the updates needed. It was comfortable, just as a beach inn should be.

Although dependable hot water and electrical circuits that didn't trip when she plugged in a hairdryer were huge improvements.

Poppy looked up. "Not having guests will seem odd. I would say quiet, but we know it won't be with Reed's crew banging around. How are our last guests doing?"

"The doctor is fine. She's going to the marina with her family to join Mitch on his afternoon coastal cruise."

"And our bookmobile lady?"

"Libby asked some odd questions." Ivy told her about the conversation.

"Sounds like she's done her homework. But you felt uncomfortable?"

"I hope she's not here to see what she might find."

The rear door slammed shut, and Shelly strode in. "Who are you talking about?"

Ivy looked up. "The librarian."

"If she's one of those searching for hidden treasure around here, I'll show her the door myself." Shelly made a face as she kicked off her sneakers. "Tell her we beat her to it. And sadly, there's nothing else here." Shelly slid her feet into the gardening clogs she kept by the back door. "We'll have to figure out how to make squillions on our own. And I'm starting with an overhaul of the vegetable garden for spring."

"I can film the process for you," Poppy offered. "I'm posting our progress on social media. I hope people will be excited to visit to see the finished result."

Shelly glanced up. "When can we start taking reservations for late spring?"

Ivy wasn't entirely sure. "I don't want to disappoint people if the construction runs longer. Old houses often have hidden problems that only surface during renovation."

Shelly grinned. "Are you saying we might find skeletons in the closet? I don't mind if they were bankers with pockets full of cash." She snapped her fingers. "Or some of those guys that ran the gambling barge off the coast during Prohibition. If the maid hid silver coins in her wall, maybe someone else tucked away gold."

Laughing, Ivy swatted her sister on the sleeve. "Come on, Shells, I'm serious about our guest."

Poppy nodded as she scraped the last of the yogurt from the bowl. "We should watch her."

"She seemed okay to me," Shelly said. "She's a librarian, not a serial killer."

Poppy shook her head. "Technically, she could be both. Highly unlikely, unless an awful lot of books go missing. That might set her off."

"Sounds like you've been reading mysteries." Shelly poked her niece in the ribs. "Like *The Case of the Lethal Librarian*. Good title, right?"

Ivy laughed at the idea. She could always count on Shelly to bring the humor.

"Maybe I'll write that someday," Shelly said thoughtfully. "As for now, I'm going to harvest more lemons and plant tomatoes." Shelly grabbed a tart kumquat and tossed it into her mouth.

"What about the spring flowers you usually plant around the perimeter?" Ivy asked.

"With Reed's workers trampling the flower beds and sawdust flying everywhere?" Shelly shook her head. "I'll wait until the construction storm passes. It's that or spend every day screaming at them."

With a chuckle, Poppy left to check on their guests, leaving Ivy with Shelly.

Shelly eyed her. "Are your instincts tingling?"

"I just have a lot on my mind." Ivy chewed her lip in thought.

"That's not what I asked, but if that's the way you want to be—"

"Libby asks a lot of questions, that's all. And her replies are vague," Ivy added.

"Maybe my book should be *The Case of the Too Curious Librarian Who Gets Wacked.*" While Ivy laughed, Shelly added, "You can take me out of the Big Apple, but you'll never get rid of my New York attitude. I adopted that, and it stays with me for good."

"You're incorrigible," Ivy said, grinning. "But I can't shake the feeling that Libby is looking for more than she's letting on."

Still, what if Shelly was right? Ivy's skin crawled as she thought about it.

8

*L*ight streamed through the music room's open doors, illuminating dust particles dancing in the air. Ivy stepped onto the protective paper covering the hardwood floors, joining Reed, who was measuring and making notes in a spiral notebook.

"Good news," Reed said. "The project is well under budget. You planned for cost overruns, so you'll have extra funds for other updates you want."

Ivy was pleased to hear this. "Then I'd like to customize some of the public spaces to improve efficiency." This was a chance to reshape the inn to update its casual beach comfort and historic elegance.

Her nephew looked up from his measurements, a pencil tucked behind his ear. "What did you have in mind for this room?"

Ivy surveyed the space thoughtfully, seeing it as it usually was in her mind's eye. Plastic sheeting covered the grand piano in the corner, protecting it from construction dust and paint splatter. Other furnishings were draped in the center of the room. The ornate fireplace and vintage light fixtures were similarly protected.

"To improve the ease of our daily tea and wine gatherings, I'd like a wall of built-ins right there," Ivy said, pointing to a blank wall. "We need cabinets to store napkins, serving platters, extra music stands, electrical cords, batteries. All the practical things we spend time searching for and ferrying around the inn when we host events. That's time lost every day for set up and clean up." Running an inn with a lean staff was all about efficiency.

Reed nodded, jotting notes. "Smart. Cabinets above, too?"

"The same." Ivy ran her hand along the wall. "I want something that feels upscale but beach casual. Guests should feel comfortable coming in with sand in their shoes but still feel like they're somewhere special."

"Got it," Reed said. "Like the rest of the house. Relaxed. Elegant but not pretentious."

The door swung open, and Shelly breezed in, her cheeks flushed. "Sorry I'm late. Just dropped Daisy at Darla's for a little while."

Ivy smiled. "How's that going?"

Shelly laughed and shook her head. "Darla was on her hands and knees childproofing when I arrived. She told me she tries to see everything from Daisy's point of view."

"That's smart."

"Now that Daisy's taking a few steps at a time, Darla's convinced she'll be climbing the bookshelves soon. So she's planning to anchor them to the wall."

"Good idea." Ivy shook her head. "Sometimes I'm surprised we survived childhood. But accidents happen. We should do the same."

Shelly grinned. "I can't wait to tell Mitch how thrilled Darla is about baby-proofing her home."

"Who would have thought she would turn into such a doting surrogate grandmother?" Ivy shook her head, still amazed at how their neighbor had changed. "You have him to thank for that."

"You did your part, too. You're the one she sued in the beginning." Shelly grinned and joined them at the wall.

Poppy appeared in the doorway and paused. "What are we looking at besides a blank wall?"

"Ivy is thinking about built-ins for storage and display," Reed said.

Noticing a faint line on the wall, Ivy took a step forward. She traced her finger along a line barely visible beneath layers of paint.

"See these outlines? There might have been furniture here before. That's about where I'd like the new cabinets."

Shelly squinted at the wall. "Old wallpaper lines, maybe?"

Reed stepped closer, running his hand over the surface. "Maybe a poor tape-and-float job. But then, everything around here shifts as the ground does."

He tapped lightly, the sound changing from hollow to solid as his knuckles moved across the wall. "Sounds solid. Must be some built-ins on the other side."

"Except there aren't." Poppy had a quizzical look on her face.

A memory of the first time she and her sister attacked a wall flashed through Ivy. "We need to check that."

Shelly broke into a broad grin. "Sure do."

Reed pulled a utility knife from his tool belt. "Since you want to cover it up anyway, I don't see why not."

"Be careful," Ivy said, her heart quickening.

"Hold on." Reed scored the drywall carefully along the faint rectangular outline. He pried an edge free.

"Don't be so slow." Shelly grabbed another tool from his

belt to help.

"Wait for me." Laughing, Ivy joined in.

Poppy whipped out her phone. "This time, I'm getting it all on video."

A section of the old drywall came off surprisingly easily, crumbling under their hands. Ivy gasped at the sight of a fine wooden edge. "Let's keep going."

They removed another section, revealing a recessed space with cabinets.

"Wow, look at that." A frisson of excitement spiraled down Ivy's spine, just as when they'd discovered the hidden art collection.

"Woo-hoo!" Shelly shot a hand into the air. "I just knew this old house had more secrets."

Eager to see what was inside, Ivy tried to open a door. "It's stuck."

"The hinges haven't worked in years." Reed examined the cabinet doors and reached for a liquid lubricant to clean them. "We'll see what the previous owner wanted to hide."

Ivy could barely contain her excitement as Reed worked.

This old house had already revealed so many treasures from its past. Letters, artwork, hidden rooms. Each discovery connected her more deeply to its history and Amelia Erickson, who loved this house.

Watching Reed work, Ivy stepped back into an oddly cold spot. Immediately, she shifted out of the way.

Amelia loved her home so much that Ivy still sensed her presence.

Not that she'd ever admit that to Shelly. Her sister would publicize the ghost angle in a heartbeat, and that might be the end of their business. Who would want to sleep in a haunted old inn?

"Any luck yet?" she asked, growing impatient.

$\mathcal{F}$resh from his morning run, Bennett slowed outside Java Beach, taking in the scene. The intricate mural on Libby's bookmobile shimmered in the morning sun. But that wasn't what caught his attention.

He wiped his brow with the edge of his "Life is Better in Summer Beach" T-shirt, surprised to find a line of people snaking around the vehicle. The bookmobile hadn't been there when he left for his run an hour ago.

Word had spread fast.

A festive atmosphere filled the air. Elderly couples with canvas tote bags chatted excitedly while young mothers bounced toddlers on their hips. A group of teenage boys Bennett would have sworn never voluntarily picked up books, leaned against a nearby wall, trying to look cool while waiting their turn.

A group of girls watched them, giggling.

Bennett grinned at the scene. Each time someone emerged from the bookmobile, arms laden with books and faces bright with anticipation, the line would move forward, and the next eager patron stepped inside.

He couldn't recall ever seeing anything like this in Summer Beach.

Bennett watched as Mrs. Hammons, his former sixth-grade teacher, descended the steps clutching a stack of mystery novels like a treasure.

Spying him, she waved him over. "Have you been inside yet? It's marvelous. She even had a new book I've been dying to read."

"Not yet." Bennett nodded toward the line. "Looks like half the town beat me to it."

"It's worth the wait, dear. When was the last time you read a book?"

He smiled at the question. "I'm usually reading budgets and resident requests."

"Then you should check out a book." Mrs. Hammons spoke as if assigning homework.

"Yes, ma'am. I believe I will. If there are any left."

Mitch emerged from the open door to Java Beach with a tray of iced coffees. His brother-in-law looked harried but pleased. "Hey, Mr. Mayor. How about one of my new spring specials? It's on the house."

Bennett accepted gratefully. "Thanks. Looks like you have a crowd."

"This bookmobile is the best thing that's happened to this street in months," Mitch said, distributing the remaining drinks to waiting customers. "Every table inside is taken. I called in Cassandra for an extra shift."

Bennett noticed that Jen from Nailed It next door had set up bistro tables and chairs outside her hardware store. Several patrons sat there, engrossed in their books while nursing coffees and pastries. Some had the hardware store's shopping bags beside them.

Mitch had also followed suit, transforming his side of the sidewalk into an impromptu outdoor cafe.

"Smart move with the seating," Bennett said. "Did you get city approval for that?"

Mitch's eyes widened. "Dude, come on. Really?"

Bennett chuckled. "Approved. It creates a nice ambiance."

"I can't take the credit," Mitch said, visibly relieved. "It was Jen's idea to put out tables and make it a party."

As if summoned, Jen appeared with her husband, George. They both wore jeans and T-shirts emblazoned with the Nailed It logo.

Jen smiled at Bennett. "Isn't this fantastic? The foot traffic has exploded."

"It's been a good morning." George gestured to the display furniture where red "sold" tags fluttered in the breeze. "We've already sold two patio furniture sets."

"And it's still early," Jen added, practically bouncing with energy. "Who knew books could be such good business?"

Bennett glanced toward the bookmobile, catching a glimpse of Libby through the side window. She was in her element, animated and dressed in what looked like a vintage-style dress patterned with tiny books. She spotted him and waved before turning back to a woman.

"The bookmobile is sure popular." Bennett stroked his stubbled jaw. "How did people know to show up?"

Grinning, Mitch explained, "As soon as I saw Libby pull up, I posted on social media. She's camera shy, so I took photos of the books and the bookmobile."

Jen folded her arms. "I guess she's one of those who doesn't want her photo taken. But those posts are getting a ton of engagement."

Bennett found that curious because most young people of Libby's age posted plenty online.

Just then, another familiar couple approached. Nan waved, her short red curls gleaming in the sunlight.

"We haven't seen this much activity on a Saturday morning since Christmas," Arthur commented, surveying the scene with evident pleasure.

"We had to check it out," Nan said. She clutched a vintage cookbook she'd apparently just acquired from the bookmobile.

"When we saw the queue forming, we opened our shop early," Arthur said. "A gentleman who came for the bookmobile wandered in and bought a fine set of vintage Hemingway books."

"Seems like a domino effect," Bennett said thoughtfully. "The bookmobile generates more business for everyone."

He watched as a young girl, no more than six, emerged from the vehicle clutching a picture book to her chest, her face radiant. Her father followed, carrying a stack of chapter books. "Daddy, can we come back next Saturday to get more?"

"We'll have to return these books then," the man replied. "After that, Miss Libby will be on her way to another town, so we can't check out others."

Bennett felt a twinge of regret as he saw the little girl's face fall.

"Everyone loves a bookmobile," Mitch said, following Bennett's gaze. "Especially the kids. What a shame we can't keep it here or offer something like that."

"Not you, too?" Bennett drew a hand over his forehead.

"Just stating the obvious, man."

A slim woman with a stylish silver-haired cut approached them. Bennett recognized Paige Wilson, owner of Pages Bookshop in the village.

"Good to see you here, Mr. Mayor." She greeted him with a firm handshake. "Quite the literary festival we're having."

"I'm surprised to see you here," Bennett said. "Isn't a bookmobile your competition?"

Paige laughed, shaking her head. "Not at all. Libraries create young readers, who then support my bookshop." She gestured toward the children eagerly waiting in line. "Libraries expand readership, develop early reading habits, and improve grades. They set up kids for success. What a shame you couldn't manage that library fiasco better."

That comment hurt. Bennett hadn't heard the budget issue called that, but he could see how residents might view it that way. "The city might reconsider filling the void in some way."

Paige eyed him with suspicion. "If you're ready to seriously discuss it, get in touch. I was sick then, but I'm feeling better and ready to serve on a fundraising committee now. It might take a few years to raise the money, but it's the result that counts."

"You make a good point," Bennett said.

A weight settled on his shoulders. Ivy had tried to enlist help, but few volunteered. Or maybe people had the chance to miss the old library now.

"Look at them all." Mitch watched another group of children skip toward the bookmobile. "I hope Daisy is as excited about books at that age."

Bennett nodded, unable to deny the evidence before him. The energy in the village this morning was incredible. People were sharing stories and laughing. The bookmobile had brought the community together.

This is what Summer Beach had been missing since the library closed.

"I should get back to the inn," he said, eager to find Ivy. "Good coffee, Mitch. Thanks."

Bennett considered possibilities as he walked. Since Summer Beach couldn't afford a library right now, a bookmobile might serve residents until it could. With some community support, it might work. It could be the first step, a bridge until they could rebuild.

He picked up his pace, energized by the idea of having a constructive conversation with Ivy about the library instead of another tense standoff. He'd told her he couldn't manufacture funds in the budget.

Yet, a bookmobile could work in the interim. Historically, many small towns provided such services while raising funds through donations, taxes, grants, or bonds to support building a library.

Of course, Ivy had been right all along. The community needed this.

10

*W*hile Reed worked on a cabinet hinge frozen by time, Ivy stepped back. "I want to see what's behind this wall."

"No problem." Reed pried another section loose and inspected the framing behind it. "This entire section is a false wall. Non-load bearing and not uncommon. In building, we add them to create storage or give a finished look to big-screen televisions."

Ivy paused as Shelly continued peeling off the drywall. "TVs didn't even exist when this house was built."

"That's hard to imagine," Shelly said. "Did they have phones?"

"We've found the old wiring," Reed said. "Anyone who built a home of this size at that time had telephones."

"Maybe they hid bars of gold in here," Shelly said, laughing.

A peculiar sensation struck Ivy. "This time, you might be on to something." Her heart raced with anticipation as the wall crumbled away, revealing more cabinetry.

Reed winced as Shelly attacked the wall with enthusiasm rather than technique. "Careful, you might—"

A chunk of drywall crashed to the floor, sending up clouds of debris. They turned away, shielding their faces.

"Oops." When the dust settled, Shelly grinned, not looking remotely apologetic. "At least we can see more now."

"Hang on. You should use these." Reed handed them painter's masks from his tool kit. Ivy saw a smile tugging at his lips. "You two are worse than my demolition crew. There's a method to—"

"Finding hidden treasures," Shelly finished for him, wedging her borrowed screwdriver into a seam. "And we're experts at that."

This time, Reed nodded. "Experts at making messes, like my dad says."

Poppy laughed, nodding in agreement. "He warned you." She stopped the recording to join in.

Reed chuckled as his sister and aunts dismantled the wall with gleeful abandon. All he could do was help them.

They worked in a flurry of dust and laughter, tearing away decades of debris to reveal the entire expanse of built-in cabinetry. The cabinets stretched nearly the entire wall length. The impressive built-in unit featured numerous compartments of various sizes.

"Just like old times," Shelly said, brushing dust from her hair. "Remember when we uncovered the entry to the lower level?"

"That was the beginning of it all." Ivy stepped back to survey their work. The cabinet doors were now exposed. "Reed, let's pry these open."

He nodded, already applying the lubricant to the hinges and working a putty knife along a door edge. "Stand back. No telling what's inside."

Shelly shuddered. "Like mice?"

"We don't have mice," Ivy said pointedly.

Reed winked at them. "Maybe because they live in here." With a crack, the first cabinet door creaked open. "Aunt Ivy, take a look."

With a tentative step, she peered into the cabinet and sighed.

"Ledgers," she said, pulling out a leather-clad book. "Looks like old accounting books." She opened one carefully, the brittle pages crackling beneath her fingers. "Household expenses. They're all labeled by year. The last one ends in 1941. Maybe that was when this was constructed."

Shelly had already moved to the next cabinet that Reed opened. "Hey, look at these." She removed a tarnished silver frame that held a portrait of a distinguished couple in an early automobile. "Look, family photos. Here's Amelia and Gustav."

Poppy opened a third compartment. "This one is full of bank statements from First Golden State Bank of San Francisco. I wonder if that exists anymore."

"And I wonder if the money is still there," Shelly said, grinning.

Ivy shook her head. "Bank accounts were probably included in the estate. I've never heard of that bank, so it's probably long gone."

They continued exploring, finding more silver serving pieces like those they'd found when they first moved in.

Ivy sorted through more documents. "These must have been important once, but they're meaningless now." She paused, thinking about the things in her life that would also diminish in importance. "I'll check the lower cabinets."

"One more shot at the gold," Shelly said.

"Here goes." Ivy knelt, excitement still tingling as she pried open a lower compartment. Inside lay a long, cylindrical object wrapped in what looked like oilcloth.

Reed's expression brightened as she carefully extracted it. "That looks like architectural plans. For this house, I'd guess."

"We have a set of plans," Ivy said. "Bennett gave them to me when I moved in."

"Maybe this set had some secret rooms," Poppy said. She gestured to a patio table just outside the open doors. "Let's unroll the plans out there."

They gathered around as Reed unrolled the architectural drawings. The wide paper was yellowed but remarkably well-preserved.

Ivy frowned as the drawing came into view. "That's not Las Brisas del Mar," she said, referring to the home's original name.

"The Summer Beach Library and Art Museum," Shelly read from the title block.

They all fell silent, staring at the detailed drawing of a building.

"Was this ever built?" Reed asked.

Ivy shook her head. "I don't think so. I've never seen it."

"Why would these plans be stashed away?" Shelly wondered, tracing a finger along the elegant facade of the proposed building.

"Amelia had her reasons for everything," Ivy replied softly. "Remember, this would have been right after the attack on Pearl Harbor. She probably sealed this the same time as the lower level, fearing an invasion from the Pacific Ocean. As people volunteered for military service and went to war, there wasn't much building going on here."

"Was invasion a real threat?" Reed asked.

"It was," Ivy said, recalling a conversation with Nan and Arthur and accounts she'd read. "A few enemy submarines cruised the California coast, attacking merchant ships and an oil field. That was probably before Amelia Erickson converted the house into a rehabilitation facility for wounded people who served."

"What an incredible history." Reed studied the plans with professional interest. "These are remarkably detailed. The design is amazing. You'd have to update the plans to current building codes, but the bones are exceptional."

Across from Ivy, Poppy peered at the drawings. "Dad will love to see these."

"Imagine if this structure had been built," Ivy added.

Her brother Forrest appreciated fine architecture. A bitter-sweet feeling washed over her as she admired the beautiful building that never came to be. She looked up at Reed. "I wish you and your father could build this for us."

"No budget, though." Shelly sighed, echoing Ivy's thoughts. "Bennett's made that clear enough."

"Wait," Poppy said suddenly, pointing to the corner of the drawing. "Look who designed it."

Ivy leaned in. "Julia Morgan." Her breath caught. "The architect who designed this house and Viola's home in San Francisco. And Hearst Castle. No wonder these plans are gorgeous."

"I've been there," Reed said. "If she worked for William Randolph Hearst, these plans might be valuable as a historical document."

"Yes, but because of her efforts." Ivy had read quite a bit about her. "Julia Morgan was a pioneering architect. She grew up in Oakland and graduated from Berkeley with a degree in civil engineering. She was also the first woman to earn her certificate in architecture from the *Ecole des Beaux-Arts* in Paris. And became the first female architect licensed in California in 1904."

"That was before women even had the right to vote," Shelly added, pressing her lips together.

Poppy shook her head. "Julia Morgan designed hundreds of buildings in her lifetime."

"Now I'm even more impressed," Reed said. "These plans have historical significance."

Ivy recalled what Libby had said about Amelia's rumored plans for a library. "Libby told me about an old article, an interview with Amelia Erickson. She mentioned her plan for a library for Summer Beach." Nan had showed her an article, too. Ivy ran her hand across the rendering with reverence. "Maybe we haven't been thinking big enough."

As she studied the elegant design, possibilities stirred within her. These plans had lain dormant for decades, waiting for the right moment. Perhaps this discovery wasn't just a glimpse into Amelia's goals but a blueprint for the future.

Shelly quirked a grin. "Don't you think it's interesting that you wanted a wall of cabinets right where Amelia had covered these up?"

"No, it makes sense." Ivy knew what Shelly was driving at. "It's what the room needs."

"Maybe Amelia's spirit led you there," Shelly said. "I wonder if she's in here with us right now, saying, 'you go, girl.'" She bumped her sister's shoulder.

Ivy laughed. "I don't think she'd put it quite like that."

"I bet she's picked up a few phrases having hung out with us." Shelly bounced on her feet. "Did I tell you there's a new clairvoyant in town? Maybe we could talk to Amelia, sort of like having a conference call with the dead."

"Shelly, stop. You're freaking out Reed." Ivy noticed their nephew's face had paled.

"It's not me," Reed said quickly. "I don't actually believe in ghosts." He exhaled and drew a hand over his forehead. "But it's my crew. Some are superstitious. There was one old house they wouldn't work on. The guys felt weird cold drafts on hot days. A couple of them thought they saw a shadowy figure. I had to hire a different crew."

"Then I wouldn't let him in Amelia's old suite," Shelly said.

Reed looked doubtful. "Which one is that?"

"My old room," Ivy replied. "And it's perfectly okay. I slept there and didn't sense anything."

"Much," Shelly added with rounded eyes.

Ivy poked her sister. Shelly didn't need to add that, even though Ivy had sensed something.

She put a hand on her hip. "Hey, Shells. Do you want Reed and his team to finish this renovation, or would you rather do it yourself?"

Shelly held up her hands. "Forget what I said. You know how I like to kid around."

Just then, Ivy spied her husband entering the music room. "Bennett is back. Wait until he sees these plans." She was excited to share their latest discovery.

"Not so fast." Shelly shook her head. "He's not going to like this. If Summer Beach has no budget for a small space, he'll go ballistic over this. You know you'll want it."

Sensing some truth in what her sister said, Ivy hesitated. "I'm not asking for anything. I'm sharing what we found."

"Wow, what happened in here?" Bennett stared at the debris in the middle of the room. "This place is a wreck. What are you all huddled about out there?"

As Shelly shook her head, Ivy rolled up the plans and tucked them under her arm. "You were gone a long time."

"After my run, I stopped by Java Beach. You wouldn't believe the crowd Libby has drawn with the bookmobile. There's a line waiting to go inside."

Shelly nodded. "Yeah, the community really wants a—*ouch*, that's my foot, Ives."

"Oh, sorry." She shot Shelly a pointed look before turning back to Bennett. "How is Mitch?"

"He's thrilled. Java Beach is having a booming breakfast run because of the crowd."

Shelly snapped her fingers. "Next to Java Beach might be a good spot for a—"

Ivy cut her off again. "Shelly, I forgot to tell you our guest is looking for you."

"I saw Dr. Kempner at the bookmobile," Bennett said. "She'll probably be there a while." He glanced at the plans Ivy held. "Those look old."

"We just found them concealed in that section," Reed replied, gesturing toward the wall. "Not for this house, but for something else."

"Let's have a look." Bennett held out his hand, his expression curious.

With a sigh, Ivy handed him the plans, watching as he unrolled them on the table. The paper crackled slightly.

"Would you look at this," he said, his voice full of appreciation. "Plans for a library and art museum."

Ivy stepped to his side, their shoulders nearly touching as they leaned over the detailed drawings.

"They seem to have been prepared after the Ericksons built this property," she explained, pointing to the date in the corner. "Looks like they were interested in building out the town."

Bennett nodded thoughtfully. "They were very civic and philanthropically minded."

His fingers traced the outline of the building, and Ivy found herself watching his hands and waiting for his reaction.

Reed peered over Bennett's other shoulder. They began discussing the space, pointing out features and dimensions.

"Doesn't look like a large library," Bennett said. "Though it's big enough for Summer Beach, even now."

Ivy looked over his shoulder, trying to imagine the building as it might have been and might still be. "I bet she planned to display some of the art we found downstairs in the museum. Or maybe showcase pieces from their private collection."

The possibilities unfolded in her mind. "Just imagine what a beautiful addition this would have been to the community."

"Sure wish it had been built." Bennett rolled the plans up and handed them back to Ivy. His eyes met hers and drew her in. "These plans are important. Keep them safe."

"I will." Ivy took the plans, her fingers brushing against his. Whatever he thought of her efforts to create a library here, he clearly admired these plans.

Reed looked back at the debris in the music room. "I'll have my crew finish the work and clean up."

"And I'll take the silver to the kitchen." Poppy picked up a tarnished platter.

Bennett took Ivy's hand, and they began to walk toward their apartment above the garage. "I was impressed with the community's reaction to the bookmobile. There was a line waiting to get in, and everyone was so…"

Ivy smiled. "Happy?"

"Ecstatic. I've been thinking about what the city would need to do to offer a bookmobile until funds are available for a permanent library. That could take years, so a bookmobile could serve residents until then."

"That's a good idea."

"And?"

She hardly dared to voice her thoughts.

"I know that look in your eyes," Bennett said, catching her hand.

"What look?"

He squeezed her hand. "You want to build Amelia's library."

"Oh, imagine if we could, darling." With her pulse pounding at the thought, she smiled at him, testing the idea.

He stopped to cradle her face in his hands. "This is what I love about you," he said, kissing her. "Even the impossible doesn't faze you."

This idea was beyond what she'd ever imagined. Beyond transforming the old beach house into an inn. Beyond the current renovation and far beyond her fundraising efforts.

Despite her husband's faith in her, she had no idea how to begin.

11

*I*vy sat at her desk by the open door in the library, the sun slanting across the room as she reviewed the monthly financial accounts. With the latest discovery still on her mind, she could hardly focus, but the work still had to be done.

The inn's finances were improving, but there was still a long way to go before she would breathe easier. The renovation had to stay within her detailed budget. She made a few notes to discuss with her bookkeeper when the phone rang.

"Seabreeze Inn, this is Ivy speaking."

"Hello, Ivy," a pleasant male voice replied. "Please connect me to Elizabeth Carter's room."

"I'm sorry," Ivy said. "We don't have anyone by that name staying with us."

"You didn't even check."

"Excuse me?"

"Do you memorize every guest's name?"

"I don't need to. We are closed for renovations."

"How about Beth Becker?" His tone was still casual but insistent. "Has she stayed there recently?"

A slight prickle of unease traveled up Ivy's spine. "No one is here by that name either. You might try the Seal Cove Inn."

There was a brief pause before the man asked, "Is there a bookmobile in town?"

Ivy's radar went off immediately. The question seemed oddly disconnected from his search for this Elizabeth person and was now related to Libby.

The coincidence was too strange to ignore.

"I have another call I need to take. Goodbye." She hung up before he could respond.

Ivy stared at the phone, feeling unsettled. She'd been borderline rude to the man. Perhaps he was only looking for information about local services. Yet, she was trying to trust her intuition more, and something about that conversation wasn't normal.

The hours passed in a blur of invoices and billing statements, yet the strange call lingered in the back of her mind.

LATER THAT AFTERNOON, Ivy heard someone singing. She stepped out of the library and onto the veranda. Libby was walking to her room, singing as she went.

"You sound like you had a good day," Ivy said, grateful for the distraction from her bookkeeping. "I'd love to hear about it."

"It was wonderful." Libby's eyes shimmered with happiness. "The bookmobile was packed all day. I helped so many children and adults find books. That's the most gratifying part of my work."

Ivy smiled at Libby's natural enthusiasm. She radiated joy, and it was contagious.

"You love your work, don't you?"

"I do," Libby said. "I love meeting people and interacting over books. It's the only time when I feel myself. I'm usually one of those awkward people who gets picked last for sports teams."

"That's not who I see in front of me. I see a beautiful young woman, strong and capable." Ivy was genuinely pleased that Libby had found such happiness in Summer Beach. "I'm glad you've enjoyed your visit and that we could accommodate you. I hope you return soon."

Libby's smile faltered. "I told people I would be back next week. Could I stay here again? I don't mind the noise."

Ivy hated to disappoint her. "I'm afraid we'll be closed for construction starting Monday. But Los Angeles is close enough for you to make a day trip, isn't it?"

"I wish I didn't have to leave," Libby said. "Summer Beach is one of the friendliest towns I've been to."

Bennett had shared his thoughts about having a bookmobile in the community, but that was only at the idea stage. There was nothing she could offer Libby with certainty.

"It sounds like you have a job waiting for you in Los Angeles," she said.

She wondered if she should tell Libby about the phone call. The caller hadn't asked for her, so it likely had nothing to do with her at all. And Libby was so happy right now.

"We've had quite a day, too," Ivy said. "We found the plans for the library and art museum Amelia Erickson wanted to build. It would have been a beautiful addition to Summer Beach."

Libby's eyes widened. "So she was serious about it. I wish I could see it built." Her expression grew wistful.

"I can show you the plans now."

Libby looked tempted. "I met some readers who invited

me out for dinner, so I should freshen up. How about later tonight or tomorrow morning?"

"Right after breakfast is fine." Ivy paused. "Are you taking the bookmobile to the village again tomorrow?"

Libby nodded. "As a service to those who couldn't make it today. Then I'll be on my way." She hesitated as a wistful look crossed her face. "Thanks again for letting me stay despite construction."

"We're glad to have you," Ivy said, and she meant it. "It turned out to be no trouble at all, and you've made many of our friends very happy. I hope you'll come through Summer Beach often."

As she watched Libby cross to her room, she saw Reed catch up to her, and they chatted for a few minutes. Although she couldn't hear what they were saying, they seemed to agree on something, and both hurried off in different directions.

Ivy wondered what that was about, and then she remembered how they'd talked last night at the family supper. She leaned against the open door to the veranda, enjoying the fresh air as she turned over ideas in her mind.

"You look like you're plotting something," Poppy said, appearing in the doorway to the library with two mugs of tea. "I figured this is one of the few times we can have a private afternoon tea. Shelly is right behind me."

Ivy accepted the steaming cup gratefully. "It feels a little odd not to have guests to entertain."

Shelly eased in with a chilled glass and plopped into a chair.

Ivy grinned at her juice cocktail. "Virgin or fully loaded?"

"Lightly loaded with just a whisper," Shelly replied. "I have to keep up with Daisy. On second thought, maybe I should make it a double and let Mitch take over tonight." She sipped a little and wagged her eyebrows. "Or maybe we'll put Daisy to bed early."

"You can hope." Ivy laughed, knowing that Shelly had earned a break. She'd been working in the garden and green-house all day.

Shelly dangled her feet over the arm of the chair. "Mitch said Libby's bookmobile was a huge success today. I hope she puts Summer Beach on her regular rotation."

Ivy sipped her tea. "I'm pretty sure Libby would stay in Summer Beach if she could."

"Really?" Poppy perched on the edge of the desk. "Maybe the community could hire her to stay on. She seems perfect for the role."

"She does," Ivy agreed. "But we don't know anything about her training or background. And funding would have to be approved by the city. That takes time."

Poppy's eyes lit at the challenge. "I could write a proposal and research grant options."

"That would be a huge help," Ivy said, remembering how much time that took. "Bennett would appreciate that, too."

. Poppy turned to her computer. "Okay, let's see where Libby worked before. I overheard her talking to someone. She let slip that she worked in Phoenix for the library system. I'll bet we can find out what position she held. It would help to include her in our proposal, and it would be easier not to have to interview people."

Sipping her drink, Shelly nodded. "Start sleuthing."

Poppy tapped Libby's name on the keyboard and pressed a key. She scanned the results. "There's no record of her. Could Libby be a nickname?"

Ivy thought for a moment. With a sinking feeling, she said, "Try Elizabeth."

Poppy tapped in the new name but still shook her head at

the results. "Nothing except centenarian obituaries. It's like she never existed in Phoenix, or anywhere in Arizona. Usually, there's some trace of a person. Social media accounts, at least. Let me try adding bookmobile to the search."

While Poppy searched in vain, Ivy told them about the phone call. "Maybe this is related, or maybe not."

Shelly was quiet for a moment. "You should tell Libby about that, Ives."

"And frighten her?" She wasn't so sure.

"Maybe she has reason to be scared," Shelly said.

Poppy leaned forward. "Or maybe we're the ones who should be concerned. What if she's a murderer on the run?"

"I'd choose something other than a bright bookmobile if it were me," Shelly said.

"Think about it." Poppy shook her head. "A mild-mannered librarian might be the perfect cover."

"Okay, enough conjecture, you two." Ivy was more than a little concerned, but she didn't want to let on. "She's leaving in the morning. If we want to consider her bookmobile for the community, she'll have to submit an application with identification. Same as anyone else who would have a city contract."

While Shelly and Poppy talked, Ivy frowned at her tea, wondering if Reed had asked Libby out tonight. Still, he knew she was leaving tomorrow, so it couldn't be serious.

As if reading Ivy's mind, Poppy pressed her lips together. "I have to warn Reed about this. He'll tell me it's none of my business again, but he's my brother, and I've been right before." She rose and hurried away.

After Shelly left, Ivy decided to take a better look at the cabinetry. She tapped a message to Reed, then got a cleaning rag and a bottle of furniture oil from the kitchen. In the music room, she ran the soft cloth over the built-ins they'd uncovered. The orange-scented oil revealed beautiful, finely grained wood.

Reed walked in. "You wanted to see me?"

She nodded. "I'm still in awe about the plans we found. Libby talked about this, even before we discovered the plans. Do you think that's odd?" But then, maybe Libby saw the same article Nan found.

"Probably a coincidence." Reed asked, "Is Libby staying over tonight?"

"She is," Ivy replied. "Why do you ask?"

Reed shrugged, but Ivy noticed a hint of self-consciousness cross his face. "She's interesting, that's all. Since she doesn't know anyone in town, I thought she might like to have dinner with me tonight."

Ivy bit back a smile. Reed wasn't usually so transparent, and she found his awkwardness endearing. "Have you spoken to Poppy?"

Reed shook his head. "Not really. I've been busy with my crew. I'll catch up with her later." Reed quickly changed the subject, gesturing toward the cabinetry. "You wanted to talk about these beauties?"

Ivy ran her hand over the old wood. "This is the kind of storage space I wanted in here. Instead of building new cabinetry, can these be restored?" The craftsmanship hidden beneath years of neglect was still lovely.

"They were well built, like the rest of the cabinetry in the house," Reed said, inspecting the doors. He ran a hand along the wood, then checked the tarnished hardware and examined the hinges. "I'm pretty sure we can," he said finally, nodding with confidence. "We should replace the hardware, though. I see some broken parts, and this room will have a lot of use."

"Then let's do that." She was pleased to see another piece of her vision fall into place.

"I have a restoration expert who does fine work on cabinetry. I'll put him on the schedule. The cost should fall well within your overage allowance." Reed made a few notes in his notebook before excusing himself to continue work.

As she watched him leave, she thought about how her nephew had neatly skirted her question about whether he'd spoken to his sister. That was between them. For now, at least.

12

*O*nce alone, Ivy opened the cabinets again. She wanted to get a better look at them, so she ran her oiled cleaning cloth over the interior shelves. The cabinets were in good condition for their age, likely because the wall had shielded them from use.

She was glad Reed had a craftsman who could restore them. Working her way across the wall, she inspected every cabinet methodically.

Ivy bent to clean the lower cabinet where she had found the architectural plans. As she swiped the cloth across the back, a paper slid out and flew onto the floor.

What's this? she thought.

Ivy picked it up, noting its sepia shade and printed handwriting. She reached into her pocket for her reading glasses—a new emerald-green pair that Bennett said matched her eyes.

The writing came into focus. This was a receipt for the plans they'd discovered earlier. It was dated November 1941. *For the Library and Art Museum.* The bottom part was torn. Before putting it aside, she absently turned over the paper.

The reverse side was covered in a flowing script, likely written by a different person.

Ivy recognized a name. It was Amelia's father, Hans.

A little farther down was a street address, and on the following line, a string of numbers divided by spaces. Probably a telephone number.

Ivy's heart quickened. Could this be the address to her father's museum in Berlin? Maybe Amelia had sent him a copy of the plans. They might have corresponded, sharing artistic and philanthropic visions.

As she stared at the address, her chest fluttered with excitement. This wasn't just a historical curiosity; this was an actual address. Was it to the museum? Or maybe to her father's home?

She remembered that Lea Martin had visited the museum. Lea was Amelia's great-niece from Germany who came to the fundraising gala and made the winning bid on the necklace Viola had found in San Francisco.

Closing her eyes, Ivy touched the jagged paper, willing guidance or inspiration from it, but she felt nothing aside from admiration for Hans. He helped his daughter Amelia save numerous masterpieces during the war. However, as Ivy and Bennett recently discovered on their honeymoon on Mallorca, Hans paid the ultimate price for this service during the war.

A thought struck Ivy. Modern technology could take her to almost any address virtually in seconds. Clutching the envelope, she hurried from the music room.

When she burst into the library, her niece was back.

Poppy looked up from her laptop. A marketing spreadsheet filled the screen. "What's up?"

"I found this receipt for the architectural plans." Ivy held up the torn paper. "There's also an address written on the back that I want to look up. I think it might be Amelia's father's home or museum. Or something else."

Poppy's eyes widened. She pushed her chair back and made room for Ivy to sit beside her. "Let's check."

"Did you speak to your brother about Libby?" Ivy asked.

Poppy blew out a puff of air, clearly exasperated with Reed. "He said he was too busy. But I'm not giving up. We have a long-standing sibling pledge. We're under oath to tell each other what we think of who the other one is dating. On the surface, I like Libby, but I feel like she's not being truthful about something."

"It's nice to have someone looking out for you." Ivy smiled at the idea. "Does that work for you guys?"

Poppy twisted her lips to one side. "It can be rough, but we're usually right about them in the end. Guys see things in other guys, and we do the same with other women. So far, it's been good, even if we don't like to hear each other's honest impression at first."

"I can imagine. Shelly and I never agreed, but then, we have completely different taste in men. Even though Bennett and Mitch are close friends, they're pretty different."

"That's for sure." Grinning, Poppy said, "Let's look up that address you found."

Ivy typed the street address into the search bar, adding *Berlin, Germany* at the end. She leaned toward the screen, holding her breath in anticipation.

The results were immediate. However, the search engine pulled up the street address in Switzerland.

"That can't be right," Ivy said, perplexed. She shook her head and reentered the information, double-checking each character and adding the country, Germany. "Same result."

Poppy frowned. "Try again."

The next time, Ivy tapped DE, the abbreviation for

Germany. Yet, the results were similar. *Switzerland.* She ran her hands over her face. This was more than a decade before Amelia had returned to Europe, with Switzerland as her last residence, so it didn't make sense.

"Choose that," Poppy said, pointing to an address that was somewhat similar in Germany.

This time, Ivy's search revealed a modern manufacturing building in Berlin. "It's not the same address, but it's close."

"Whatever was there might have been lost in the war," Poppy said, squeezing Ivy's shoulder. "Or torn down later to modernize the area. It's been years."

A wave of disappointment washed over Ivy. Another possible connection to the past had slipped through her grasp. But she didn't give up easily.

"One more time," she said. Yet again, the screen flashed the address in Switzerland.

"Wait a minute." Poppy leaned in. "Enlarge the street image and swing the view around."

Ivy tapped and zoomed in. "It's in a business district, but that can't be right. Amelia's father lived in Berlin." She sighed, leaning back in her chair. "I guess too much time has passed. Some things we might never know."

"It was worth a try, Aunt Ivy." Poppy brightened and switched tabs on her laptop. "Want to see the marketing plan for the inn? I have some great ideas for the grand reopening."

"Sure. We're all looking forward to that."

While listening to Poppy's enthusiastic pitch about social media posts, ad campaigns, and submissions to travel bloggers, Ivy's mind wandered back to the receipt. Something about it still disturbed her.

After Poppy finished, she asked if Ivy and Bennett had plans for dinner. "Mom and Dad told me to invite you for supper. They know you're packing up the place."

"Thanks, but I'd planned to stay at home since this is the last night we have guests. But we'll take them up on that offer next week."

After Poppy left to visit her parents' home, Ivy turned her thoughts back to the mysterious address. She tried again but failed to find anything online.

Always worth a try, she thought, tacking the slip of paper to the corkboard behind her computer for inspiration.

WHEN IVY WOKE the following day, Bennett had already left for his run on the beach. She rolled out of bed and stretched, taking her time. It was Poppy's turn to lay out the breakfast buffet, and since they only had two guests now, it wouldn't take her long. After dressing, she strolled across the car court, past Libby's bookmobile, and into the kitchen.

Poppy wasn't there, so she continued to the dining room.

Reed's deep voice floated through the hallway. "These design elements are similar to this house."

Ivy paused at the entrance to the dining room, where everyone gathered around the old set of plans for the library and art museum.

Libby looked particularly interested, but Poppy seemed upset, her lips pressed into a thin line.

"What architectural style do you call this?" Libby asked.

"A blend of Spanish Colonial Revival and Mediterranean styles," Reed replied.

"I heard Amelia Erickson marked a large sum of money for the construction," Libby said with a smile. "Do you know anything about that?"

Ivy stepped inside. "The estate was settled and closed several years ago." No wonder Poppy was on edge.

Libby whipped around, clearly surprised. Her wide-eyed gaze looked innocent enough.

Yet, after her conversation with Shelly and Poppy yesterday, Ivy hadn't slept well. She didn't trust Libby until she knew more about her. Questions from strangers about finances and money were red flags. And from the looks that Poppy and her brother were exchanging, their talk hadn't gone as planned.

Ivy gave Libby a pleasant smile; she was still their guest, after all. "You're up early. Will you be getting on the road soon?"

"She couldn't leave without seeing these plans," Reed said. "I told her all about them last night at dinner. They're incredible."

Libby's cheeks colored slightly, and she glanced down at her hands.

Ivy turned to Reed. "How nice of you to join her bookmobile readers at dinner. It must have been fun."

Reed raised his brow in surprise. "Libby, I didn't know you had plans."

"Everyone understood once I explained why I couldn't make it," Libby said quickly. "They all know you, so once they learned you'd asked me out, they were happy for us. And they shared the sweetest stories about you."

It was Reed's turn to look a little embarrassed. "I'm sorry we disappointed them. Had I known, we could have joined them. And don't believe everything they say about me."

Her mind racing, Ivy headed straight to the coffee urn for liquid reinforcement. *Not a good situation*, she thought, slightly panicked for Reed.

She turned back to Libby. "Traffic can be heavy on Sunday returning to Los Angeles. You should probably leave sooner than you'd planned so you can be fresh for your interview tomorrow."

"That's true," Reed said, touching her shoulder in a protective gesture. "I hope you'll return soon."

"I'm planning on it," Libby replied, beaming at him.

Oh, dear, Ivy thought. *Reed looks far too interested.* She glanced at Poppy, who was clearly holding back her comments. Her niece would have plenty to say later.

Libby glanced at the time. "I should get ready for my visit to the village."

"Are you parking by Java Beach again today?" Reed asked.

"Mitch asked if I would. He told me the bookmobile is great for business, and I'm welcome anytime." Libby gave him a timid smile. "I've heard that a lot. People love books, especially if they don't have a local library. Many small communities don't, so I feel like I'm providing a real service."

"I admire what you're doing," Reed said, his gaze transfixed.

Her nephew was falling for Libby, even though there were cracks in her stories. Ivy refilled her cup and tried to sort out her issue with Libby.

"I should be going soon," Libby said, glancing nervously at Ivy. "I've enjoyed my stay here. I wish I never had to leave."

"You brought a lot of joy to our readers," Ivy said. "I know they'll look forward to seeing you again soon." She meant what she said, and she liked Libby.

As for trusting her, that was another matter entirely.

13

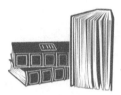

*a*fter giving Poppy the rest of the day off, Ivy began packing items in the ballroom to keep them out of harm's way. Shelly was spending Mitch's day off with him and Daisy.

Bennett had joined her to pack until he received a call from his sister asking if he could pick up his young nephew as they'd been delayed in traffic, so Ivy was on her own.

Ivy was still packing when she heard the front door open. "Hello," she called out.

"It's me," Libby said.

"Oh, hello again." Ivy was surprised to see Libby returning after opening the bookmobile in the village again. "I thought you were on your way to Los Angeles."

Libby bit her lip. "The interview was canceled."

"How unfortunate. I'm sorry to hear that." Something seemed off, especially when she thought of a major library system canceling an interview on a Sunday for the following day. "What are your plans now?"

The younger woman looked uncomfortable. "Would you mind if I stayed here a few more days?"

Ivy wished she could help her, but she had already made one exception. "I'm sorry, but the construction project is ramping up first thing in the morning. We can't risk guest injuries. Along with the noise and dust, I'm afraid it won't be pleasant. That's why we're closing."

Libby looked a little lost. "Is it okay to park the bookmobile on the street for a few days?"

What a bold question, Ivy thought. "It's not up to me to say, but I'm afraid that's against city ordinances. However, there's an RV campground where you can park. It's only a few minutes away, and I can give you the address."

Libby nodded as if that would have to do. "Do you mind if I come back to visit? Reed will probably let me. I love watching renovation shows on TV, and this is the real deal."

"He might, but I'd rather you didn't. It's for your safety, and we can't risk the liability. You might trip or touch a hot wire and sustain an injury. We must take precautions." A live wire had already shocked Ivy, though it hadn't been serious.

Libby nodded again, looking dejected, although she made no motion to leave.

Ivy studied the young woman. She hadn't wanted to confront Libby, but now she left her little choice. Maybe there was another story than the one Ivy imagined.

She took a step toward Libby. "I've been thinking that you might not have arrived here on a whim. I have an idea you planned your arrival to coincide with the construction."

It would have been easy to track their construction plans. Shelly and Poppy had been covering that on their social media.

A guilty look washed over Libby's face. "I know what you

think, but I'm not a treasure hunter. I didn't come here to find or take anything from you."

"Then what is it you want?"

Libby hesitated, her face flushing from embarrassment. "I want a chance to start over, be safe, and become part of a community." Her voice dropped to a whisper. "I just want to make friends and belong somewhere."

Ivy wasn't sure how to respond. Libby's reaction wasn't what she expected. Her expression was raw and vulnerable, leaving little doubt she was telling the truth at last.

"You never had a job interview in Los Angeles, did you?"

Libby shook her head. "I wanted people to think that my skills were in demand and that another library wanted me. I've been unemployed so long that I've forgotten what it was like to be valued enough to hire." With shame burning in her eyes, she looked down at her hands. "I'm sorry for misleading you."

Ivy guided Libby to an overstuffed chair and sat across from her. Ivy's heart cracked for the young woman. She remembered how she'd felt after Jeremy died and how difficult it had been to reenter the workforce after so many years, the occasional tutoring of art students notwithstanding.

She also recalled how lonely she felt. Many friends didn't know how to act around a new widow. So their calls became fewer and farther between. The dinners she and Jeremy had once enjoyed with other couples ceased entirely; she became an extra person who threatened to upset the natural balance.

What she didn't realize then was that she'd gained her freedom. Later, she thought of that as a consolation prize that allowed her to do whatever she wanted with her life on her terms.

Ivy noticed tears welling in Libby's eyes. "Thank you for sharing that. I sense you've had some difficulties in your life, and I'm sorry we started off wrong."

Wiping her eyes, Libby managed a shaky smile. "Me, too," she said in a small voice. "I never wanted to hurt any of you."

"From what I've seen," Ivy continued, "you've brought happiness to many people in the community. And having the freedom to travel and create your income is what many people dream of."

"I loved that in the beginning," Libby said, beginning to recover her composure. "Being alone, even though I was surrounded by children and adults, became lonely after a while. And I want to rest sometimes but have no place to call home."

"You're seeking a home now, and that's the first step." Ivy leaned forward on a hunch. "How did you know about Amelia Erickson's plans for a library here?"

"I was following Shelly's blog," Libby said, sniffing back her tears. "I became so intrigued that I began searching for Amelia Erickson's history. I also had a part-time job transferring ancient microfiche to digitized files for a small newspaper. That's how I discovered a reference to her in an old article."

"What was the article about?" Ivy asked.

"It was an interview about Amelia working with Julia Morgan, the architect who designed her homes here and in San Francisco. She told the journalist she had engaged the architect to create plans for a library and art museum she would build in Summer Beach to honor her father."

That made sense, given that Hans was a museum director. "Do you have a copy of that article?"

Libby brought out her phone and showed Ivy the photo she had taken of it. "I can print it for you."

Ivy squinted to read it without her glasses. "Please. The writing is too small for me to make out." She stared at Libby, piecing together the backstory that was shifting into focus, although there were still missing parts. "Besides discovering the architectural plans for a library, what else did you hope to find here?"

Libby rocked a little in her chair. "Summer Beach sounded like a place where I could feel safe."

Ivy peered at her. "Safe from what?"

Looking flustered, Libby pressed a finger to the corner of her eye and shook her head.

Her reaction troubled Ivy. She wondered if she should mention the phone call. "Even though it sounds like you've had a grand adventure, I imagine traveling alone across the country can be frightening at times."

Ivy laced her fingers and waited, but the young woman didn't seem ready to elaborate. Whatever Libby was concealing had been heartbreaking to her.

"I can help you research more about Amelia's plans for the library," Libby said, veering off the topic. "That's what I do. I was a research librarian."

Ivy recalled the old newspaper article again. "If you researched the Ericksons, did you know we'd find the plans?"

"I hoped you would, like you'd found other things here." Clasping her hands tightly, she paused to catch her breath. "If you built the library, I could help. I thought I could get a job here, that's all."

Ivy was more curious than ever now. Libby had done her research, made plans, and executed them. She had dared to dream, traveled to Summer Beach, and was willing to work. Ivy had to respect her actions, which seemed rational when put in perspective. This plan must be the best of Libby's options.

Ivy touched her chin in thought. "Where did you say you went to school for your training?"

"I went a few places and finally graduated from a state university."

Another vague answer. "You can trust us, Libby. If you want to help with a project, you should know that I expect honesty. That's important to everyone in Summer Beach. This is a small town. And there are more than a few people who've overcome adversity and built new lives here."

Wiping another errant tear that spilled onto her cheek, Libby nodded. "I want to trust people."

"Then, why don't you start by telling me your real name?"

Libby's face grew ashen. "How did you know?"

Ivy stared back at her, weighing her thoughts. She didn't want to spook the young woman, especially if she was in trouble or needed help.

She tried a different approach. "Is there more you'd like to tell me? Many guests have confided in me, so there isn't much I haven't heard."

Libby frowned, and a heavy sigh of relief escaped her lips. "I'd like that." She glanced around. "Can we talk on the beach?"

Touched by her reaction, Ivy nodded. Whatever was troubling Libby, she preferred to speak privately. Looking down, she noticed Libby's cowboy boots under her flowing cotton dress. "I have a basket of flip-flops for the beach by the back door."

Libby followed her, and they changed their shoes for the beach.

Pausing by the door, Libby said, "I haven't told anyone besides my best friend about this."

Ivy didn't know what she was referring to, yet she sensed the young woman needed reassurance. "I won't share what you tell me." She hoped she could keep that promise. She would try unless Libby was involved in something illegal or harmful. But she didn't get that feeling from her.

The overwhelming feeling Ivy sensed from Libby was fear.

14

"*I* should start with my real name," Libby said, walking beside Ivy on the beach. "It's Elizabeth. In school, I went by Elizabeth or Beth, but my mother always called me Libby. After she died, I just wanted to hear that name again, so after I left Phoenix, I became Libby again. Libby the librarian seemed to flow better. I also reverted to Becker, my mother's maiden name, because my father never wanted anything to do with me."

"I'm sorry you lost your mother." A thought occurred to Ivy. "Isn't there a library app by that name?"

A small smile tugged Libby's lips. "That makes it even easier for people to remember me."

Ivy slowed her pace and waited for Libby to continue. Rushing the young woman wouldn't help.

The tide was going out, leaving patches of wet sand that gleamed in the spring sunshine. Nearby, families with children worked on sandcastles, and seagulls glided above receding waves.

Finally, Libby spoke again. "I haven't been completely

honest with you." Her voice was quiet, almost lost in the sound of the waves. She stopped walking and faced the ocean. "I'd like to find my people in Summer Beach and help the community with library services. But that's not the reason I left. It was personal, and that's why I've kept moving."

"I sensed that. Many people move for personal reasons."

"I left Phoenix because I broke up with my boyfriend," Libby said. "I was studying for my master's degree in library sciences when I met him. It wasn't long after my mother passed away in an accident, and I guess I needed someone. All my friends were getting married and having babies, so I figured we would, too."

"Why didn't you?"

"Dolph was fun at first, but he would go off on emotional tangents. He would get so angry that it scared me. His anger wasn't directed at me, at least not initially. Looking back, I think he began to change when I gave up my apartment and began planning our wedding. First, he blamed his outbursts on me and then on the stress of his job. Or the person who cut him off on the highway, or the overworked waitperson. It was never his fault."

"Did you ever seek counseling?"

"Dolph wouldn't go, and I didn't want to go without him. He became more and more abusive. Emotionally at first, then physically."

She winced and twisted a strand of hair around her finger, a nervous gesture Ivy had noticed. "I filed a restraining order against him and left. I couldn't stay there anymore."

Ivy's heart ached for the younger woman. "That must have taken a lot of courage."

"I don't feel brave," Libby said, shaking her head. "Most days, I just feel scared. I'm afraid he'll track me down. He's been trying." She kicked at the sand lightly. "That's why I bought the bookmobile. It wasn't just because I love books, though I do. It was a way to keep moving, to not stay in one place too long."

"That was smart."

"I bought it on a whim from a bookstore chain that used it for promotions. They were closing and auctioning everything, including the bookmobile, which they had trouble selling because of how it was outfitted. But it was perfect for me, and I had a little money my mother left to me."

"Do you think Dolph is still looking for you?" Ivy asked. She thought of the call she'd received. She would tell Libby, but she wanted to hear her story first.

Libby shrugged. "Maybe. I blocked him on social media and later changed all my social accounts, along with my phone number. I don't like to post my photo anywhere. Still, my friend who knows him says he's obsessed with getting back at me. That's the friend who painted the bookmobile for the bookstore. I don't want to put her in an awkward position, so I don't tell her very much."

Libby slid off her flip-slops and dug her toes into the sand. "Even though I have a few friends in Phoenix, I don't want to return. Too many sad memories there. I want to start a new life, but I wonder if it's too late."

"Too late?" Ivy echoed, surprised.

"I turned thirty last month," Libby said as if that explained everything. "All my friends back home are married with kids. They have careers, houses, and husbands. They have goals and direction." She wiped tears from her eyes. "Five years of my life with Dolph, gone. I made a terrible mistake in waiting, thinking he'd turn around."

"You were also grieving and needed to feel loved."

They had reached a large, flat rock. Ivy sat down and patted the space beside her, inviting Libby to join her.

"Each time he'd blow up, he would promise to make it up to me," Libby said, sitting down. "He would do something lavish, change a little, and life would improve for a little while. But the next time he lost control, it would be worse until finally, I ended up in the emergency room one night." She squeezed her eyes against the memory, and her voice grew softer. "I know he needs help, but I lost all respect for him. I couldn't do it anymore."

"It wasn't your fault and that was no way to live." Ivy nodded, understanding flooding through her. "You're not responsible for his happiness, only your own."

"I know, but I am so afraid that I missed my only chance at having a family." She dipped her chin. "Even Reed is younger than I am. He doesn't know I'm older yet."

"A couple of years doesn't make much difference." While Ivy had been concerned about Reed's interest in Libby, she wouldn't judge the young woman anymore. She had been through enough.

Libby ran a hand over her hair. "Starting over by myself seems so hard."

"It can be daunting if you're used to having parents or a boyfriend who helps you." Ivy turned to face her. "But you're not alone. Summer Beach is friendly, and trust me, it's never too late to start over. I did it in my forties. My husband died, so my sister and I moved here. We didn't have many options, but we managed."

Libby looked intrigued. "How long ago was that?"

"Just a few years. Summer Beach, Bennett, and the inn are all part of my second act." Ivy smiled. "And don't worry about being on a timeline. Life isn't a race. You'll know when it's right. But I think you already know that."

"I love my little bookmobile, but it's fairly cramped to live in." Libby gestured vaguely toward the neighborhood behind them. "I don't know if I'll ever find a home again."

"You will," Ivy said. "It might not be what you imagine, but if you're open to possibilities, you might be surprised. Summer Beach has a way of helping people find what they need, even if it's not what they were looking for."

She looked down at her feet, wiggling her toes in the cool sand. "I love it here. The people are so kind and accept me as I am. An awkward librarian with funky thrift-shop clothes."

"Everyone here has a story to tell. You'll be surprised." Those stories weren't Ivy's to tell yet, but if Libby stayed, she would learn them soon enough. "Someday I'll take you to Thrifty Threads. It's my favorite resale shop. Just steer clear of the prom dresses."

Libby smiled at that. "I don't know what I would do here."

"Exactly what you've been doing with the bookmobile. I've also been thinking about holding a book festival here to raise funds for temporary library services like a bookmobile. And eventually, to raise enough to build a new library."

Libby's lips parted in awe. "I would love to help with that."

Ivy's mind was full of possibilities. "I'll see what I can do."

"If I stay here, what if Dolph finds me?" Libby asked suddenly, her voice small.

"You can't run forever, but you won't face him alone." She reached over and squeezed Libby's hand, still reluctant to tell her about the phone call. "I have good friends here who can help. Imani is an attorney who runs the flower stall in the village. She's dating Chief Clarkson, our head of police. You can talk to them."

A flicker of hope crossed Libby's face. "Do you think they could help with the restraining order? Make sure it's valid here?"

"I can introduce you to Imani now," Ivy said. "She's at her

flower stall nearby. Why don't you stay another night at the inn?"

"Are you sure?" Libby asked, sounding hopeful.

"The work won't start until tomorrow morning. You might as well be comfortable tonight."

Ivy gestured toward the village. "Come on. Let's go look at some flowers."

Libby brushed sand from her feet and put on her flip-flops. They strolled up from the beach onto Main Street.

"There it is." Ivy motioned to a flower stall bursting with color.

Buckets of fresh flowers lined the sidewalk, their sweet fragrance permeating the air. A hand-painted sign read *Blossoms*.

A tall woman with dark braids twisted into a crown atop her head was arranging displays of sunflowers, roses, and peonies. Her tie-dyed sundress was as vivid as the flowers surrounding her. She looked up as they approached.

"You're just in time," Imani called out. "I was about to close." She put down her clippers and wiped her hands on her apron.

Ivy placed a hand on Libby's shoulder. "Imani, this is Libby. She's been staying at the inn with her bookmobile."

"You're famous," Imani said with a warm smile, extending her hand. "I've heard about you from half the town. They sure love your bookmobile."

Libby shook her hand, looking slightly overwhelmed. "It was a good turnout."

Deciding to be direct, Ivy said, "Libby has a legal question. I thought you might advise her."

Understanding flickered in Imani's eyes. Before becoming a florist, she had been one of Los Angeles's most respected attorneys. Her keen observational skills hadn't dulled with her career change.

"Legal questions are my specialty." Imani's smile widened as if Ivy had mentioned a fondness for cake. "I'm closing soon. Why don't you wait, and we can talk?"

Relief washed over Libby's face. "You wouldn't mind?"

"Not at all." Imani turned the sign on her stall to *Closed* and began to draw the plastic curtain.

Ivy and Libby helped her carry in the remaining buckets, filling the small space with even more fragrance and color. As Imani finished, Ivy leaned in close to Libby.

"Would you like me to stay with you?" she asked quietly.

Libby hesitated, then shook her head. "I'll be okay now. Thanks for letting me unload my problems on you."

"Are you sure?"

Libby blinked and nodded. "I need to do this myself. I'm long overdue."

Ivy understood. The first step toward reclaiming power was to face the issues and ask for help if needed.

Imani approached, untying her apron. "All set. We can talk on the bench over there."

"Just a minute," Ivy said to Libby. "There is one more thing I should mention. I wanted to wait until after you met Imani. I received a call yesterday." She went on to tell her about the conversation.

Libby's face paled. "That had to be Dolph. I knew this was too good to be true. I don't know if I can stay here."

"You shouldn't have to run," Imani said. "We'll figure it out together. Let's talk." She nodded to Ivy.

Imani would know what to do. Ivy gestured toward the marina, where Bennett had taken Logan earlier after picking him up. "My husband should be finishing his work on the boat, so I'll join him now. Call if you need me."

Imani lifted her chin. "Tell him I said hello. And I'll take Libby back to the inn after we've had a chance to talk."

Feeling lighter after talking to Libby and understanding what she wanted, Ivy turned toward the marina. Imani would advise her, and soon Libby could close that chapter of her life. She also admired the young woman's ingenuity with the bookmobile.

In the distance, she saw Bennett on the deck of his boat, cleaning and repairing the craft for the season. His vintage yacht was his happy place, and they enjoyed taking it out on the water.

She would surprise him, she decided.

15

*B*ennett wiped his brow with the back of his arm, careful to keep the varnish on his brush from dripping onto the deck. The afternoon sun glinted off the ocean waves, and the air was fresh. He loved being on the water. Rubbing his shoulder, he put down his brush.

His nephew Logan had helped him today on the boat before his parents picked him up a little while ago. He'd asked Ivy if he should return to the inn with him, but Ivy told him to take Logan out on the boat. Kids didn't like packing. He appreciated that.

The rumble of an approaching engine caught his attention. He glanced up to see Mitch's charter boat easing into its slip across the dock.

"Hey, Mr. Mayor," Mitch called out, waving at him.

A group of about ten people talked and laughed as they disembarked. Many stopped to shake Mitch's hand or clap him on the shoulder. Bennett could hear fragments of happy conversation carried on the cool breeze.

"Best day we've had so far. Glad we found Summer Beach."

Bennett nodded to himself. Between Java Beach and his coastline charters, Mitch was good for Summer Beach and tourism. After helping the last of his customers onto the dock and pointing them toward the parking lot, Mitch secured his craft and headed Bennett's way.

"Looking mighty good," Mitch said, gesturing to the freshly varnished wood.

Bennett set his brush across the top of the can. "Successful charter today?"

Mitch's grin widened as he stepped onto Bennett's boat. "Small family reunion. Good people." He leaned against the cabin. "You know what they were talking about for half the trip back? Libby's bookmobile."

Bennett groaned. "Not you, too."

"I know you're probably tired of hearing about the bookmobile and our lack of a library, but you had to see it all day. People just kept coming, and many came back today with friends. Word got around fast."

Bennett sighed and sat down on the bench seat. "All of this has been a sore subject at my house."

"Ivy's still pushing for the library?"

"It's been a source of contention between us," Bennett admitted, rubbing the back of his neck. "I wish the city had the budget to build and staff it properly, but we just don't. Even with funds the state and federal governments would kick in, which isn't much. The numbers don't work."

"What about donations?"

"That's a big ask." He shook his head. "Most of our community donors have committed their budgets for the year. So I feel twice as bad about those old architectural plans. That building would have been perfect for Summer Beach. Ivy would love it."

Mitch nodded, commiserating with him. "Shelly told me about it. Man, I wish the Ericksons had built that. You have no idea how much Shelly has been talking about it."

"I can imagine." Ivy had drafted Shelly into the library effort. Bennett scraped his stubbled chin in thought. "What if the city could host the bookmobile more often?"

Mitch bumped his fist. "That would make a lot of people happy." His gaze shifted over Bennett's shoulder. "But you should tell Ivy that. Here she comes. And I'd better get back to work."

Bennett turned to see Ivy approaching on the dock. As sunny rays brightened her face and the highlights in her hair, his heart tightened with admiration for the woman he'd married. She went after what she wanted and had a knack for figuring out how to make it happen. If only it were within his power to approve what she wanted.

"I didn't expect to see you here," he said, reaching for Ivy's hand to help her onto the bobbing craft.

"I was nearby." She told him about Libby's revelations. "Now we know what she was hiding and why."

"Glad to hear it. She seems like a smart, decent person."

"Maybe I was being too protective of Reed."

"Family looks out for each other."

She started to sit down, but Bennett scooped her into his arms. "Wet varnish," he said, kissing her.

She laughed. "Best excuse I've heard to steal a kiss. You know you can kiss me anytime, right? We're doubly married."

"No, really. That section is wet." He showed her his work. "I'm getting this craft shipshape for the summer."

"I'm glad you're taking the time to do that." She dipped her head. "By the way, thank you for helping me pack at the house earlier today. I know it's my responsibility to manage my team, so you don't have to pick up the slack, but I appreciated it."

"It's being with you that's important. If that means helping you at the inn, then I'm all in. No pun intended." He grinned and smoothed a wisp of hair from her face.

He led her to another area where they could sit and look over the ocean. Putting his arm around her, she settled beside him.

She inched closer and touched his hand. "It's been a long time since we were out on the water together."

"Too long. We'll take the boat out soon." Bennett felt a pang of regret. Between his mayoral duties and her renovation projects, they'd both been busy.

Ivy drew her eyebrows together. "Are we settling into that marriage routine where people stop doing the fun things they once did?"

"I don't intend to." He took her hands and kissed them. "But we don't have to do anything special to keep our love alive. I cherish every day with you." He paused, recalling how quickly his first wife had fallen ill, and then she was gone. "But point taken. *Carpe diem.* Let's plan a nice getaway after the construction."

"I'd like that. Hearing Libby talk about her travels made me want to explore."

Bennett took a deep breath. "About the library issue," he began.

Ivy squeezed his hand and looked at him with a guarded expression. "Are you sure you want to talk about that?"

He kissed her forehead, reassuring her. "Libby's bookmobile gave me an idea. We might not have the funds for a library yet, but I've reviewed the budget. The city has some discretionary funds, so we can likely manage a stipend for Libby to visit Summer Beach more often for our residents."

A smile played on Ivy's lips. "That would be a good start, and she would probably appreciate it. Is this your way of thinking outside the box?"

Bennett chuckled; he often said that to Ivy. "The idea of a private bookmobile is different, but it solves a need here. Do you think she would be open to the idea?"

Ivy's eyes shimmered. "Her dream is to stay here. And I have another dream."

Bennett knew what she was getting at. Although many libraries across the country were scaling back, this was still worth a try. Summer Beach needed this. "If we adjust budget allocations and raise private funds, we could make progress toward the end goal. Would you be willing to introduce Libby and present the bookmobile proposal to the council?"

The smile that spread across her face lifted his heart. "Of course I will. And I have all sorts of other ideas."

Bennett laughed. "You have an inexhaustible supply, and that's part of what I love about you. Tell me what you're thinking."

"People were thrilled to visit the bookmobile." Her words tumbled out in her excitement. "So, what if we create an annual book festival here in Summer Beach? Sort of like our art fair. In the beginning, we could build it around Libby's whimsical theme. We could invite authors for book signings and have entertainment. Make it a real destination event."

Bennett grinned at her enthusiasm. He recalled what Mitch said about the family treasuring the small-town experience. "I like the sound of it already."

"There's so much more we could do," she said, her green eyes sparkling. "We could organize fun events for the kids and invite booksellers and food vendors. Nominal admission fees, booth rentals, and donations would go toward a permanent library. But we should comp Paige's booth. She reopened her bookshop after the earthquake, and it's the only one in town. We need to keep her in business, too."

"These are good ideas." Bennett thought a literary festival was particularly appealing. He imagined Summer Beach's streets filled with book lovers and vendors. "This would bring more tourism into Summer Beach. The business community would be happy about that."

"We'd start small, but I know it will grow," Ivy said. "And it would fulfill the Ericksons' vision for our town, even if it takes us a few years to get there. We should do it as soon as possible. I'll pitch it to Shelly and Poppy."

Bennett nodded in thought. "The council will like the tourism angle, and an annual fundraising event creates a path toward a permanent library without breaking the budget." He leaned forward and kissed her. "You've got this, my darling. Put me down as volunteer number one at the book festival."

Bennett felt the tension that had wedged between them for weeks finally dissipating.

She threw her arms around his neck. "I've always known we were a great team."

"The best. Sometimes we just have to work through difficulties."

"That makes the results even sweeter." She threaded her arms around his neck and kissed him. "Maybe I haven't told you I love you enough lately."

Bennett thought his heart would burst at her words. "Same here. I know it, even when you don't say it. I hope you do, too."

Filled with love for his wife, he smiled at her, his mind filling with ideas on how they could make it all up to each other. "How about we take the boat out one afternoon this week, just the two of us? I have some time off I can take. After all, I am the mayor."

"I would love that." Ivy leaned her head against his shoulder. "I miss our private time together."

"Then how about we have a gourmet platter in the treehouse tonight?" The balcony they'd added onto the rear of their over-the-garage, former chauffeur's apartment was surrounded by palm trees that swayed and swished in the ocean breezes. He'd surprised her with an outdoor sofa and furnishing. "I can offer a lump of burrata cheese with aged balsamic vinegar, a loaf of crusty bread…"

"Mmm, I'd like that." She ran her fingers along his neck. "I'll add Marcona almonds in olive oil, mandarin oranges from our trees, and sliced veggies."

Bennett's heart thudded at the thought of this romantic evening alone with his wife. "I saw a bottle in the fridge of that sparkling rosé cava we had in Mallorca. Fancy that?"

Ivy nodded with a sigh. "It's a date, darling."

He leaned in to kiss her. They deserved this time together. Now, all they had to do was gain council approval and organize the festival. He was thankful their relationship was getting back on track because their lives were about to get even more complicated.

16

*I*vy rose early the following day, even before Bennett. Having promised to send her bookkeeper bank statements for her financial reports and tax return, she threw on a pair of jeans with a lacy blouse and went straight to her office.

Bennett stopped by on his way to City Hall. "You were up early." He bent to kiss her.

"Bev needs my bank statements and cash expenses. I need to gather all the documents, so I figured I should do this before Reed's construction crew arrives. The noise level will escalate fast, making it difficult to concentrate."

"You might have to work elsewhere," Bennett said.

"If it gets bad enough, I'll do that." She kissed him goodbye before he left.

After finishing her task, she assembled the digital documents in an email to her bookkeeper. *I believe this is everything, Bev. Let me know if you need anything else.*

Once sent, she closed her email program, and her gaze settled on the old, torn receipt she'd tacked to her corkboard.

Something about it nagged at her. She stared at the address scrawled on the back with a fountain pen and the string of numbers underneath.

She unpinned the slip of paper, studying it again. The address didn't match any location in Germany. *Why would Amelia have had an address in Switzerland at that time?*

And why didn't she build the library and art museum in Summer Beach?

For a dreadful illness to have struck down such a vibrant, determined woman in the middle of her life was a tragedy. What else might Amelia Erickson have accomplished given more time?

Ivy shook her head, realizing that question applied to everyone on earth. *Carpe diem*, as her husband said just yesterday. Seize the day, every day.

What if everyone lived like that?

She typed the address into her search engine again, and once more, it brought up a business district location in Zurich. This time, Ivy clicked on the street view and zoomed in.

As the image came into view, her lips parted.

"It's a bank," she whispered, leaning closer to the screen.

She clicked through several links, scanning for information. The bank was still in operation. In fact, it was one of the oldest financial institutions in Switzerland and had been in business since the late 1800s.

She picked up the torn paper again, looking at the string of digits she had assumed was a telephone number.

Then she thought of the bank statements she'd just emailed to her bookkeeper. She ran her fingers over the numbers as if divining their meaning.

What if these numbers are an account number?

The possibility sent a thrill through her. The Ericksons might have had a bank account there.

It wasn't implausible. Amelia and Gustav had traveled extensively in Europe before the war for art acquisitions. They had connections and resources.

Switzerland had been a neutral territory leading up to and during the Second World War. A quick search on the computer confirmed this. However, it also seemed that it was illegal for German citizens to have Swiss bank accounts during the war, even punishable by death.

Ivy shivered at the consequences. She wondered if that applied to those living outside of the country.

But that was a long time ago. Amelia had returned to Switzerland to live at the dementia care facility until she died. Everything would have been included in her estate.

Outside, the sudden sound of jackhammers jangled her thoughts.

Reed's crew was right on schedule. Ivy pressed her palms to her ears as she looked through the open door. They were breaking up concrete to make repairs. The ear-splitting cacophony reverberated through the house, making the old windows shudder in their wooden frames.

"This is impossible." But necessary. She would bet her last guest wasn't sleeping through this racket.

She reached for her phone and tapped a quick text to Libby: *Good morning! Need coffee and quiet? Meet me at Java Beach.*

The reply came immediately: *On my way.*

Ivy also texted Poppy and Shelly before shoving her note-book into a canvas satchel and heading out. She took the beach path to avoid the construction also taking place in the front.

Once away from the inn, the noise of the jackhammers receded. Ivy exhaled with relief at the rhythmic sound of waves washing against the shore. In the distance, she saw the bookmobile parked outside of Java Beach.

Libby was waiting, her cotton dress fluttering in the breeze. The younger woman waved when she spotted Ivy approaching.

Libby greeted her and opened the door to the coffee shop. "Now I understand why you were concerned about me staying longer. Reed's crew is so intense. I threw everything into my vehicle and shot out of there."

"Breakfast is on me for that." Ivy queued up in the line of people waiting for Mitch's coffee and breakfast specialties.

Everything smelled delicious. With beach reggae music playing in the background, Mitch managed the coffee bar while his employees took orders and ran the kitchen. When he saw Ivy, he nodded to her. "Shelly is on her way here with Daisy."

Ivy was glad to hear that. "It was too loud to work at the inn."

Just then, her phone dinged with a message from Bennett. As she read it, she smiled. He'd kept his promise.

While they waited for their turn, Ivy turned to Libby. "How did your meeting with Imani go?"

Libby's shoulders relaxed. "Very well. She's so smart. She came up with a plan, and she alerted Chief Clarkson. As long as my ex is out of my life, I'll be happy."

"That's good." Ivy had been worried about that. Especially since Reed seemed to have fallen for Libby. She didn't want him to be in danger.

They ordered mocha coffees and breakfast croissants for the table and found a place to sit. The doors were open to the beach, and sunshine streamed in, chasing the morning chill.

While their steaming coffee cooled, Ivy focused her thoughts. "Now that Imani is going to help you, there's an idea you might be interested in."

Libby leaned forward, her expression alert.

Ivy gestured toward her phone. "Bennett just confirmed that the city has some funds it could dedicate to your bookmobile service for residents. You could still visit surrounding communities every other week if you wanted, and there is a budget to buy new books, too. Would that interest you?"

Libby blinked a few times. "For real? I'd love that."

"As a contractor to the city, you'd need to fill out an application." Ivy paused. "I hope that's not a problem for you."

"I was only hiding from my ex. I have a resume, references, and can order my university transcripts."

"That's perfect," Ivy said. "You'll have to make a presentation to the city council, and Bennett says they're eager to meet you. Are you up for that?"

"This is my dream come true," Libby replied, pressing a hand to her heart.

Ivy smiled at her response. "I hope you're ready for a bigger dream. Summer Beach needs a library, and I'd like to make that happen. We plan to host an annual book festival and fundraiser to build the library Amelia Erickson envisioned."

Libby's face lit with excitement. "I'd love to volunteer."

"I think you could do more. We'd like you to help organize it." Ivy held up a hand before Libby could interrupt. "The community would pay you for your time, of course. It could be part of your contractor agreement with the city."

A smile spread across Libby's face. "When I worked at my last library, I participated in literary events and festivals. I was also the liaison for the friends of the library fundraising group, so I have a lot of ideas I can share."

Ivy was glad to hear that. From the first step into Libby's bookmobile, Ivy could tell she was a skilled librarian. She'd observed her knowledge and love of books and saw how well she connected with the public. Her experience in events and fundraising was a bonus.

"Thank you for this opportunity," Libby said, her eyes shining with gratitude. "I won't let you down."

Ivy picked up her mug and tapped Libby's. "You're on your way to being part of Summer Beach. I think the community will be lucky to have you."

"Do you think I might have a shot at being part of the library when it's built?"

Ivy appreciated the younger woman's ambition for service. "I think you'll have plenty of time to prove yourself."

Grinning, Libby sipped her coffee. "This means I'll be able to stay at the campground for a while. Chief Clarkson says it's gated and has security, so I'll feel much safer there. Maybe I can get a small place soon."

"Did you meet our Chief of Police?"

"Imani introduced us. Chief Clarkson saw Imani in the village. He said they'll keep an extra eye on me with regular patrols."

Despite the reassurance and noticeable relief, Ivy still detected a note of lingering concern, which was expected. She hoped Imani would work quickly to help Libby put the past behind her.

"If you'd like, I can help you practice your presentation before the city council. Many people want to see you stay in Summer Beach."

"I've pitched projects before," Libby said, folding her hands. "I appreciate your support, though."

Ivy was glad Libby was getting the help she needed from Imani. She saw how enterprising and hard-working the younger woman was.

Just then, Shelly's voice rang out. "Hey, hey, double trouble has arrived." She whisked toward them with Daisy on her hip.

Poppy hurried behind them. "She means them, not me."

"Oh, hey." Shelly grinned. "Then that makes us triple trouble."

"Have a seat," Ivy said, smiling. She made room at the table for everyone. "I ordered breakfast for all of us."

Shelly plopped down with her little girl and brought a bib and a banana from the diaper bag. "Thanks. Daisy is always hungry."

Poppy leaned her laptop bag by the chair and sat next to Libby. "This was a good idea to come here. It's impossible to hear yourself think at the inn. My brain's been jackhammered to mush."

Ivy laughed, nodding. "I'll check in with Reed to see how it's going. He said he'll call me if anything is urgent." She pressed her lips together, grinning at Libby.

Shelly narrowed her eyes. "What are you cooking up, Ives? I know that look. Spill the tea, girl. What's going on?"

"If all goes well, and I'm sure it will, Libby will be staying in Summer Beach with her bookmobile."

"That's great news," Poppy said, congratulating Libby. "How did you manage that?"

"Bennett worked it out," Ivy replied. "And that's not all. We're going to start an annual book festival." She quickly outlined the concept to Poppy and Shelly. "Libby will be part of the team, and she's planned events before."

"A literary festival in Summer Beach?" Poppy's eyes sparkled. "People here will love that. And it will probably draw visitors."

"That's what I'm counting on." Looking up, Ivy saw Mitch approaching, his tray laden with food.

"Make room for breakfast." Mitch placed the tray in the middle of the table. "Hey, babe," he said to Shelly. "I brought

Daisy's favorite, too. Scrambled eggs just the way she likes them. I let them cool off first."

"Da!" Daisy exclaimed when Mitch put the plate in front of her. She plunged her little hands into the eggs and shoved a handful into her mouth. "Mmm!"

"Oh, Daisy-cakes," Shelly said, whipping out a napkin while everyone laughed. "You eat with such gusto."

"We should all enjoy our food as much as she does," Mitch said, chuckling. "A cappuccino is calling my name." He kissed Shelly and Daisy on the cheeks. "See you later, sweethearts."

Watching Mitch be so loving toward Shelly and their little girl brought a smile to Ivy's face. She'd been worried about her sister's choices in men for years, but Shelly and Mitch were a good match. She hoped Libby would be as fortunate here.

They all began to eat, chatting about ideas for the book festival as they did.

"When are you thinking of holding this event?" Shelly asked. "I hope we don't have to wait until the inn is complete."

"We have more time now before the inn reopens," Poppy said, reaching for a blueberry muffin. "Let's plan it now and start small. How about holding it next month?"

Ivy nodded, her mind racing with logistics. "If we involve the city, which we should, we might use the main beach. I'm sure we could do enough to generate interest and some funds."

Libby shook her head. "If the wind blows, that much sand wouldn't be good for books. I have to be careful of that in the bookmobile."

"Good point." Shelly wiped Daisy's chin. "How about the new park at the old Seabreeze Shores Airfield?"

"Excellent idea," Ivy said, nodding. "Libby could park her bookmobile on the old runway the park is built around. Let's check on that."

Libby's eyes brightened. "I know several top authors who

might participate on short notice, too. They have incredibly supportive fans, and I can hardly keep their books in."

"Alright, next month it is." Ivy gazed around the table at faces mirroring her excitement. Sometimes the best things happened when you didn't overthink them.

"Let's do this," Shelly said, swaying with Daisy.

Ivy opened the calendar on her phone. "Poppy, will you check the community calendar and find a date that doesn't conflict with other events?"

"On it." Poppy pulled her computer from her bag.

Ivy flipped to a fresh page in her notebook. "Let's brainstorm fundraising ideas. What else could we do besides charge nominal admission and vendor booth fees?"

"What about a read-a-thon?" Libby suggested. "It's like a marathon or a walkathon. People pledge donations for pages read. Teachers might even give kids class credit. That way, everyone feels involved."

"I love that." Ivy jotted a note to contact the principal and teachers she knew in Summer Beach. Her mind was racing with possibilities. "How about a Blind Date with a Book sale?"

Shelly rested her chin in her hand. "Reminds me of my dating app disaster. What is that?"

Poppy laughed. "People wrap up their favorite books with a few tantalizing clues on the outside and sell or auction them. Buyers choose based on the description without knowing the title."

"I like it," Shelly said between bites of her croissant breakfast sandwich. "That's way better than my blind dates were. At least with a book, if you don't like it, you can close it and walk away."

"Got it." Ivy scribbled more notes, her handwriting growing messier with speed.

Libby leaned in. "A story time for grown-ups with beach blanket readings from authors."

"Bookmaking for kids," Shelly said, holding up a hand. "Not the betting kind. The coloring kind."

Ivy made a face. "I figured."

"How about a banned books trivia contest?" Libby added, "With books like *To Kill a Mocking Bird* and *The Great Gatsby?*"

Ivy looked up in surprise. "On the list, for sure."

Shelly drummed her fingers. "Everyone likes a bake sale."

"Sounds good, too." Poppy looked up from her computer calendar. "The last weekend next month is available. Should we go with it?"

They all compared their calendars and agreed. It was the only open date for months.

Ivy held up her hand. "All in favor of supporting the first annual Summer Beach Bookfest, raise your hand."

Along with the others, Shelly shot up her hand. "The Bookfest is on."

Optimism surged through Ivy. *This will work.* The festival would introduce people to the bookmobile and the library fundraising campaign. It was a step toward progress for the community. They could plan this while Reed and his skilled trades brought the inn into the new century.

Ivy read off at their growing list, and those around the table volunteered to manage different tasks.

As they were discussing more ideas, Ivy's phone rang, interrupting their planning session. Reed's name flashed on the screen. Her nephew rarely called unless it was necessary.

"Everything okay there?"

Power tools sounded behind Reed's voice. "I found something you'll want to see right away. Can you come now?"

"What is it?" she asked, her chest tightening.

"It's better if you see it. How soon can you make it?"

"Give me ten minutes." She closed her notebook. "I'm leaving Java Beach now."

Poppy leaned forward. "Is everything alright?"

"Reed found something strange." Ivy tucked her notebook into her bag. "But you can all stay here and keep talking."

"How strange?" Shelly asked, cleaning Daisy's hands with a wipe. "Like 'I found a weird nest of spiders' strange or 'we found a body and need to call the police' strange?"

Ivy shuddered. "I hope it's neither one."

"Do you want us to come with you?" Poppy asked.

Ivy hesitated, then shook her head. "Let me see what's going on first. I'll let you know."

WONDERING WHAT REED HAD DISCOVERED, Ivy hurried back to the inn, her sneakers slapping the sidewalk in triple time. As she neared the house, she slowed, gasping for air. She pressed a hand to her throbbing heart. Now wasn't the time for a cardio workout. What was wrong with her?

She paused to catch her breath. Hyperventilating in the street wouldn't be a good look for the mayor's wife.

Take it easy. Pressing a hand to her forehead, Ivy prepared herself for what awaited her.

The inn was more than a hundred years old. Had Reed found structural instability that would double the cost of repairs?

Or were Shelly's comments more accurate? She had heard of skeletons found in old structures. Or maybe he'd unearthed Indigenous artifacts or dinosaur tracks. Her stomach lurched at the potential delay any of these discoveries might cause.

If the inn didn't reopen in time, her cash flow would suffer. She would make do with less income, but she didn't expect anyone else who worked there to do that.

Not anymore.

Shelly and Mitch had a baby to provide for now. Poppy was building a life, and the part-time housekeeper and book-keeper also depended on their wages. And Sunny still needed financial help while she was finishing her graduate program.

Someday, her youngest would support herself, but that day wasn't here yet. Thankfully, Misty was self-supporting with her acting career. Her eldest daughter was so busy she rarely had time to visit, though they spoke a few minutes nearly every day.

Her forehead felt damp. Was this a panic attack?

No. The sun was warm, and she'd been racing, that was all. Whatever Reed found, well, she would handle it. Just as she always had.

But maybe it is.

She drew a deep breath and resumed walking at a slower pace until she reached the house.

As she approached the front door, footsteps exploded behind her. Spooked by her thoughts, she whirled around.

Poppy was out of breath from running. "We decided we can't let you walk into a potential disaster by yourself, Aunt Ivy."

Behind her, Libby toted Shelly's baby bag, her cowboy boots thudding on the stone walkway.

Shelly was last, with Daisy clutching her neck gleefully at the excitement. "All for one and one for all. That's how we roll, Ives. Hope I didn't scare you by talking about spiders and dead bodies. Although they would be long decayed."

Ivy had to laugh. "Only a little. I'm glad you're here."

"Maybe it's just a water leak," Poppy said brightly. "We've had plenty of those. They're not too bad."

"My vote is on raccoons in the attic." Shelly shuddered. "Or rats."

Ivy shook her head. "We have guest rooms up there now."

"Not above your place over the garage." Shelly grinned and bounced her little girl.

"You're still awful." Ivy wrinkled her nose at her sister's flippant remarks.

Daisy squealed with delight at the face Ivy made, and they all laughed.

Shaking her finger, Ivy said, "If you don't watch out, she's going to grow up just like you."

"I can't help it." Shelly laughed and swatted Ivy's shoulder. "Is that so bad?"

"I hate to say it, but I hope you never lose that." Ivy meant it, though she still poked her sister. "Come on. We might as well face whatever it is." She gestured for them to follow.

Ivy turned back to the grand old structure, scrutinizing it for any visible signs of disaster. Unable to contain herself, she burst through the front door, her heart hammering against her ribs again. "Reed?" she called out, her voice echoing through the foyer.

"In your office."

Ivy rushed down the hallway toward the library where they worked. The others were close behind.

Wearing jeans and work boots, Reed stood in front of her desk, his usually calm demeanor heightened with anticipation. He held something in his hand.

She rushed forward. "What is it?"

Reed held up an old slip of paper, yellowed with age and torn at the top. For a moment, his attention was drawn to Libby, and he smiled at her before continuing.

"Hope you don't mind my snooping around in here, Aunt Ivy. I had to see if this lined up." He aligned what he'd found below the paper she'd tacked to the corkboard until the torn edges meshed.

"They fit," she said, even more curious now. *A perfect match.*

"Like Cinderella's shoe," Shelly added in awe. "What does it say?"

Reed handed the paper to Ivy. "You should read it."

She took the paper from him with trembling fingers. Reaching for the reading glasses on her desk, she cleared her throat, preparing to read the faded fountain pen script. "It says, 'Funds on deposit for the Summer Beach Library and Art Museum.'"

Her breath caught. "Oh, my goodness," she whispered. *That string of numbers.* She looked up to those surrounding her. "This is proof that, once upon a time anyway, funds were designated for Amelia's vision."

Shelly's eyes widened. "Could they still be there?"

"Highly doubtful." Ivy smiled wistfully, her chest warming at the thought. "That was such a long time ago. I don't know why this makes me so satisfied, but it does. It confirms another dream of Amelia's that I want to fulfill."

She lowered the paper. Not just *want* to fulfill; no, she felt utterly compelled to. Perhaps by the presence that still lingered here.

Not that she would admit that, especially to Shelly.

Poppy dipped her chin. "That's because Amelia Erickson had noble ideas for this area she loved."

Libby spoke up, her eyes flashing with excitement. "This aligns with her quote from that article I found."

Ivy nodded slowly, recalling her conversation with Nan and Arthur weeks ago. Twice confirmed now. Three times if she counted their discovery.

There was no doubt in her mind. Though decades in the process, Summer Beach would have its library someday.

Amelia Erickson would see to that.

And so would Ivy.

*B*ennett squinted against the bright sunlight as he lined up his putt. The eighteenth hole of the Summer Beach Municipal Golf Course lay before him, a deceptively simple-looking par three hole. The Pacific Ocean created a stunning backdrop beyond the green that rivaled the exclusive Torrey Pines golf course south of them. A breeze carried the scent of salt water and freshly cut grass, rippling the sleeves of his polo shirt.

"Don't choke now, Mr. Mayor," Clark Clarkson called out, his booming voice tinged with friendly mockery. "Your entire political career could hinge on this twelve-footer."

Bennett shot the police chief a wry smile. "Thanks for the added pressure, Clark. Just what I needed."

He took a deep breath, steadied himself, and swung. The ball rolled smoothly across the green, curving slightly with the contour before dropping satisfyingly into the cup.

Bennett executed a quick bow. "And that, gentlemen, is how it's done."

"Pure luck," Boz grumbled good-naturedly. He pushed his

weathered Summer Beach Planning Department cap back over his thick silver hair. "You couldn't make that shot again if you tried."

"Want to bet?" Bennett picked up his golf ball to challenge him, but Hal stepped between them with a laugh.

"Let's save the rematch for next week." Hal, the most casually dressed of the four despite being the wealthiest, slapped Bennett on the back. "Nice putt, though. You're improving."

Bennett bumped his fist in appreciation. "There's always room for improvement in golf."

"As in life," Clark added.

"I won't argue with that," Bennett said. "Speaking of life, how's Imani doing with Gilda at her home?"

"She hardly sees Gilda, but Pixie is running the house." Clark laughed and shook his head. "Imani loves dogs, though. Good thing, since Pixie has been stealing and stashing things again. She's a miniature mastermind criminal."

Boz lined up his putt. "Hope you never have to go up against her."

"You got that right." Clark folded his arms. "Make us proud, Boz."

The other man swung, but the ball veered just shy of the hole. A collective gasp rose from the men as they commiserated with him. "There's always next week." Boz grinned and tapped it in.

They returned to the golf cart, Boz taking the wheel while Clark loaded their clubs. Bennett settled into the back with Hal, enjoying this brief respite from his mayoral duties. These Thursday afternoon golf games were a way to maintain friendships while keeping abreast of what was happening in Summer Beach.

As they cruised along the cart path toward the clubhouse, Hal leaned back, his designer sunglasses reflecting the ocean view. "What's the latest on the inn renovations? Carol mentioned she drove by yesterday, and it's looking impressively underway."

"Coming along well," Bennett said. "The structural work will soon be completed, and then it's down to finishes and furnishings. Ivy is managing the process well, and Reed is a rockstar contractor, like his dad."

"It's pretty generous of you two to open the public spaces to the community," Hal said. "Doesn't that infringe on your privacy? I can't imagine having people wandering in and out of your home all day."

"It's an inn, so that's expected, and we like serving the community." Bennett shrugged, watching a red-tailed hawk circling above the bluffs. "Part of the deal for the property's preservation is maintaining public access to certain areas, given the inn's historical significance."

"I enjoy the steady stream of guests," Bennett continued. "At times it's a very full house, especially without a library or other community meeting areas for residents. Ivy and her team manage the logistics, but more often, they're acting like traffic cops. We have book clubs, students with tutors, children's story times, people working remotely on laptops."

"So that's where people have gone since we lost the library. I've also noticed you can hardly get a table at Java Beach anymore." Hal raised his brow. "Doesn't that impact the ability to host events like weddings and reunions for paying guests?"

"It has. Still, it's what we agreed to." As a music producer, Hal was quick to understand the business implications.

"But that was before all the library patrons had to transition to the inn," Hal added. "Sounds chaotic."

"It can be," Bennett admitted. "I wish we could have

funded a new library in town. It would take the pressure off the inn and give the community what it really needs."

He glanced at Hal, then quickly added, "I'm not angling for donations, by the way. You've already contributed generously to the preservation fund."

Hal waved a dismissive hand. "I wasn't thinking you were hitting me up, though I'm open to the idea. The arts are important to Carol and me. That fire in the adjoining space was bad luck for the library."

Clark took in the course. "Doesn't seem fair that we still have a great golf course, and the kids are scrambling for books and places to study."

The cart bounced as Boz navigated a rut in the path. He glanced at Bennett. "You found a temporary solution, right? I heard about the bookmobile."

Bennett nodded. "I managed to locate some discretionary funds to contract for a part-time bookmobile. It's not ideal, but it will help the community. I'm pretty sure the council will agree."

Clark turned in his seat. "That bookmobile was a hit. When it was parked outside Java Beach last weekend, there was a line every time I drove past. I'm glad to welcome Libby into the community. She seems to know her stuff."

"She does," Bennett agreed. "Ivy has already started planning an annual book festival to raise funds for the library."

"That will take a while," Hal said.

"She's thinking long term." Bennett told them about the old set of plans for a library and art museum they'd discovered in the house. "Reed knows an architect who can update them to code."

Boz cleared his throat, his expression thoughtful as he steered the cart into the parking area. "You know, there's an empty site just off Main Street that might be available. It's part of a large estate that's been in probate for a long time. It's a good location that's within walking distance from most of the village."

Bennett raised an eyebrow. "The old Gutierrez parcel? I heard about it from a real estate colleague, but I didn't think it was on the market."

"It's not, officially," Boz replied, easing the cart to a stop. "But word is the family's ready to sell once the legal issues surrounding the estate are settled. Might be worth keeping an eye on."

The men climbed out of the cart and gathered their golf clubs. Bennett considered this information, mentally calculating what properties like that were going for these days. Even with his real estate background, he knew the numbers wouldn't work with the city's current budget constraints.

Hal seemed to read his mind. "You might want to broaden your thinking when it comes to fundraising. A capital campaign could work if you get the right people involved." He paused, then added casually, "Carol might appear at a fundraiser if she's available. She has a new tour coming up. Next year, we would consider a more substantial contribution."

"The immediate need will be to stock the bookmobile. The librarian who runs it, Libby, has been running it as a private venture."

"Why is that?" Hal asked.

"She lost her job at another library during cutbacks but loves what she does. Pretty genius, if you ask me."

"I'll call Tyler," Hal said. "The least we can do is help stock it until other plans are developed. Libraries serve a vital role, and it's an embarrassment that we don't have one." He shook his head. "Carol and I struggled when we were young. I spent a lot of time studying in a library, needing the quiet space I couldn't find at home. And folks over fifty like me need books to keep their minds active."

Hal was right. For every year that passed without a library, kids might fall behind in their studies. Young mothers need the story time break to get out of the house. And small business owners need the wealth of information and resources to support their families and employees.

It wasn't that Bennett didn't think Ivy could manage this effort. It was a question of time.

She was right to be upset. Many small towns were losing their libraries, and he didn't want Summer Beach to be among them.

"I appreciate that, Hal. Really. Let me talk to Ivy about the festival they're planning. Maybe we could expand it into something larger."

Clark clapped a hand on Bennett's shoulder. "Just let me know when and where. The department can help with security and logistics."

"And I can fast-track any permits the library might need," Boz added. "It's for a good cause."

As they walked toward the clubhouse, Bennett felt lighter. He'd come to the golf course looking for a break from problem solving. Instead, he found allies in a challenge that had been troubling him and Ivy for months.

Sometimes, a mayor's work took place in unexpected locations, like the back nine of a golf course on a sunny afternoon.

He didn't want to take anything from Ivy's efforts or risk her thinking he doubted her abilities.

Far from it.

He hoped she'd take this news in the spirit of cooperation for the good of the community. They still had a long way to go before the new library was built.

18

*I*vy could hear the construction crew arriving in the car court as she dressed. Over quick bowls of cereals in the cozy kitchen of their quarters over the garage, Bennett told her about his golf game, what Hal had offered about the library, and the lot Boz mentioned.

While she digested this news, he leaned against the counter, peeling an orange. He handed her a slice. "I hope you don't mind me dipping my toes into the deep waters of your business."

Ivy smiled at his thoughtfulness. "Come on in. If you start drowning, I'm a certified lifeguard."

She'd once felt like she was the one drowning—drowning in debt, lack of experience, or demanding guests. But since then, she'd gained experience and learned to accept help wherever she could find it.

She popped the fresh orange slice into her mouth. "I should call the probate trustee to see if he knows anything about a reserve account for the library and art museum Amelia planned."

Outside, the hammering began. *Thunk, thunk, thunk.*

"Come with me to the office," Bennett said, raising his voice. "I know him, and we can call from there."

Ivy appreciated this. "You're officially part of the team." She kissed him and took his hand.

Taking the rest of their fruit, they rushed out and climbed into Bennett's SUV for the short drive to City Hall.

After greeting Nan and Boz on their way in, Ivy sat on the other side of Bennett's desk in his office. He closed the door, though she could still hear the muffled sounds of the city administration at work—phones ringing, printers humming, people discussing municipal matters.

Bennett leaned forward. "Mind if I make the call since I know him?"

"Let's put him on speaker so we can both talk." After Bennett's real estate partner had become ill, her listing passed to Bennett, so he represented the trust as the selling agent.

Ivy perched on the edge of the chair, tapping her fingers as she watched him dial the number.

As he dialed the number, he gave her a reassuring smile that did little to calm her nerves.

"Hello, this is Mayor Bennett Dylan from Summer Beach." Bennett pressed the speaker button, introduced Ivy, and summarized the issue. "It's regarding the Erickson estate."

Resting her arms on the desk, Ivy leaned in to listen to the conversation. The lead attorney and trustee Bennett knew was on vacation in Hawaii.

"This is Pierce Grainger. I worked on the Erickson case as well. How can I help you?"

Bennett glanced at Ivy before responding. "We're inquiring about the possibility of an old Swiss bank account associated with the Erickson estate. Specifically, accounts that might have been designated for the Summer Beach Library and Art Museum."

There was a brief pause on the other end. "Swiss accounts? No, there was nothing like that in the estate. We did a thorough inventory of all assets at the time of Mrs. Erickson's passing. No foreign accounts of any kind were listed. She kept her banking relationships in San Francisco."

Ivy's shoulders slumped, but then she straightened again as a thought occurred to her. "But then, there might not be," she said, loud enough for Pierce to hear. "What if the account was opened before or during the war, and the information was lost or forgotten when Mrs. Erickson developed Alzheimer's? It wouldn't have been part of the known estate. Or what if it had been bequeathed to her from her father?"

"That's possible, I suppose," Pierce said slowly, though his tone suggested skepticism. "But extremely unlikely. We were quite thorough."

"Would it be possible to investigate?" Ivy was unwilling to let go of the possibility so quickly. "We've found documentation suggesting funds were specifically set aside for a library and art museum, along with what appears to be a Swiss bank address and what might be an account number."

Another pause, longer this time. "You could try, or we could look into it on your behalf. But I should warn you that Swiss banks are notoriously private. Without the proper documentation and proof of connection to the account holder, it's nearly impossible to access information, let alone funds. Especially after all this time."

The unspoken message was clear. *Don't get your hopes up.*

"I understand," Ivy said. Disappointment crowded in on her. "Thank you for your time."

Bennett ended the call with a few more pleasantries, then

turned to Ivy. Her face must have betrayed her feelings because he reached over and squeezed her hand.

"It was always a long shot." His tone held a note of apology.

"Do you think I'm letting that call deter me? That was his opinion, not mine. I have other ideas." Standing, she straightened her shoulders with determination. "I'm just getting started."

His face shone with admiration for her. "Bravo. What's next?"

"I need to think." She picked up the laptop bag she had grabbed on their rush from the inn. "See you back at the house for dinner. Unless you'd rather go out."

"Everything is getting fairly dusty at the house." He stood and took her in his arms. "Your choice."

"I'll make a plan." She kissed him before leaving.

IVY ARRIVED at the Oceanview Cafe and looked around. "Table for one," she said, giving her friend a hug.

Hallie seated her with a knowing smile. "You look like you could use some peace and quiet." She led Ivy to a corner table with the best ocean view. "This renovation is turning you into a refugee."

"A very grateful one," Ivy had replied, sinking into the chair.

"Coffee?"

"Bring it on, please."

"Are you expecting anyone else?"

Ivy shook her head. "Shelly and Poppy are planning a book festival to benefit a new bookmobile and, eventually, a library."

Hallie's face lit. "That's wonderful news. We were devastated when the library was destroyed. We sometimes drive to another one, but it's a little too far to just pop in, especially with our little ones. Let me know if there is anything I can do to help support the cause. I know what it's like to lose everything in a disaster, so I'd be happy to host a fundraiser here for it."

"Thanks, I'll let you know." Ivy would make a note of that. It was good to know the project had community support.

Hallie and her husband had come here after losing everything in a hurricane in Houston. They opened Oceanview Cafe last year. Hallie specialized in California and Pacific Rim fusion recipes, which meant plenty of mango, curry, avocados, and fresh fish. She bought her seafood every morning from family-owned fishing vessels.

The clatter of dishes inside the cafe punctuated the rhythmic sound of waves, and the aroma of simmering lunch specials floated outside. Ivy sat at her favorite table on the patio and opened her notebook.

The mid-morning lull between breakfast and lunch meant she often had the outdoor space to herself, so she could make phone calls with few interruptions. While she liked Java Beach, it was always busy with little privacy. That's where Shelly, Poppy, and Libby were right now.

Having quiet time to think was a small mercy after days of endless construction noise at the inn. However, she still checked in with Reed to see if he had questions.

"Here you are," Hallie said, serving her a cup and leaving the thermal coffee carafe on the table. "Stay as long as you like. It's nice to have your company."

Ivy poured a little cream into her coffee. "Do you have any tables open tonight?"

"For you, of course. How many in your party?"

"Just the two of us. It's date night." Ivy decided on a time, and Hallie made a note of it before returning to the kitchen.

As Ivy gazed out at the sapphire expanse of the Pacific Ocean, her mind returned to the possibility of a dormant Swiss bank account. She couldn't shake the thought, despite the trustee's skepticism. She would have to determine if an account existed and then try to prove if Amelia or her father intended to direct those funds to a library.

That was asking a lot.

But she couldn't shake the feeling that she was supposed to follow this thread, however tenuous it might seem. She needed a healthy dose of luck, of synchronicity.

As she thought about this, she doodled, sketching clovers in her notebook. Four leaves, for luck.

Who would know about Swiss banking laws? Or dormant accounts from years past? She sketched a bank building with a question mark on its façade. There must be someone who could help navigate this foreign landscape.

Just then, a seagull swooped down to perch on the patio railing. The bird cocked its head and stared at her as if delivering a message.

Ivy stared back and picked up her pencil to sketch the white bird. Mariners often believed gulls were harbingers of good news; likely they were weary sailors looking for land. Others believed the birds embodied the spirits of their fellow adventurers soaring over the seas.

After a while, the seagull lifted off, spreading its impressive wings.

If that bird had meant to deliver a message, she hadn't received it yet.

She returned to her notebook, flipping through pages of notes about the renovation, book festival plans, and now this mystery. Her thoughts drifted to the people she knew with international connections.

Suddenly, she sat up straighter.

"Raquel," she murmured, reaching for her phone. "Of course."

During their honeymoon trip to Mallorca, Ivy and Bennett befriended Raquel and her brother Carlos. As it turned out, their grandfather had worked alongside Amelia's father during the war. They were part of the network that had saved countless artworks from Nazi destruction. If anyone might have insight into European banking from that era, it would be someone with connections to that world.

Ivy checked the time. It would be evening in Mallorca, but she remembered that Raquel and her family typically ate dinner late, often not until nine or ten at night.

Worth a try, she thought.

She scrolled through her contacts until she found Raquel's number, and after a moment's hesitation, she pressed dial. The international ringtone sounded strange and distant.

"*¿Diga?*" came Raquel's voice, warm and musical even in a single word.

"Raquel? It's Ivy from Summer Beach, California," Ivy said, refreshing her memory.

"Ivy, what a wonderful surprise. How are you, *mi amiga?*" Raquel's delight carried across the thousands of miles separating them. "I hope you're planning another visit."

"I'm well, and I wish we could say hello in person, but Bennett and I are in the midst of a major renovation at the inn." Ivy relaxed at the genuine warmth in Raquel's voice.

"Oh yes, the beautiful old beach house by the sea. How is it coming along?"

"Slowly but surely. We're at the noisy stage with jackhammers and power tools from dawn till dusk." She asked about

Raquel's brother Carlos and told her that Bennett would love to keep in touch.

"Maybe we'll visit when the inn is ready."

"We'd love to see you," Ivy said. "You know, we've made some fascinating discoveries along the way."

Raquel gasped. "More paintings?"

"Not this time. Instead, we found the original plans for a library and art museum that Amelia Erickson commissioned but never built. It's an incredible design and would have been stunning." She told her about the famous architect and what having a new library would mean to Summer Beach.

"How intriguing. Why not build it now?" Raquel sounded decisive. "Such a treasure should not remain only on paper."

"We're trying to figure out how to make that happen," Ivy replied. "The city doesn't have the budget, and we're working on fundraising ideas." She paused, then decided to dive in.

"Actually, that's why I'm calling. We found something else. A paper with what appears to be a Swiss bank address and possibly a bank account number. A note indicates Amelia, or her father, set aside funds specifically for this project. I wonder if the account was overlooked when she developed Alzheimer's later in life."

There was a thoughtful silence on the other end. "This is very interesting," Raquel finally said. "Sometimes, my grandfather spoke of families who deposited their money and valuables in Swiss banks during those terrible years. They were considered safe havens, and most were able to retrieve what they had safeguarded, but not always."

"Why would that have been?"

"If the account holder died or lacked the necessary identification, it could be a problem. Many people lost their papers during imprisonment or relocation."

"Do you know if it's possible, or even likely, that such an

account could still exist?" Ivy held her breath, hoping for some confirmation that she wasn't chasing a dream.

"It is definitely worth pursuing," Raquel answered firmly. "I know of several cases where families recovered funds and belongings, even decades later. The Swiss designed their banking system precisely for privacy and security. If the account existed but was never closed, there is a good chance it still does."

A renewed rush of hope surged through her. "That's encouraging."

"The difficulty, of course, is proving your right to access it," Raquel continued. "The same privacy laws that protected the assets make them challenging to claim. But not impossible, especially if you have documentation connecting Amelia to the account."

"We have a paper with what looks like the bank's address and a number that could be an account number," Ivy explained. "And we found a note specifically mentioning funds designated for the Summer Beach Library and Art Museum."

"That is more than many start with," Raquel said. "You must follow this trail, Ivy. If nothing else, it is a fascinating historical puzzle. And if it's successful? Imagine what it would mean for your community."

"I will," Ivy said, already thinking about next steps. "Thanks, Raquel. I knew you'd understand why this matters so much."

After promising to send photos of the finished inn, Ivy ended the call. She stared out at the ocean, watching sunlight dance across its surface.

The seagull returned, alighting on the railing again.

"Well, hello you. Did you come to sprinkle fairy dust over me?"

Once again, the bird angled its head at her and stared.

Who to contact next? she mused, tapping her pencil. The Swiss bank itself seemed like an obvious choice, but from what she'd read, they would be unlikely to release information unless she went through legal channels.

She brought out her laptop to research more.

After replenishing her coffee cup, Ivy had another idea. *Viola in San Francisco.*

The older woman knew a lot of professionals who might have the knowledge she needed. Maybe she would know of someone.

That possibility was worth a phone call.

Once again, the seagull lifted off, soaring into the skies. And then, she thought of another person who might have even more intimate knowledge.

19

*T*he umbrella over Ivy's table at the Oceanview Cafe cast dappled shadows across her notebook as she tapped her pencil, waiting for an international phone call to connect.

However, the call went straight to voice mail, so she left a message for Lea Martin, Amelia's great-niece. As she hung up, a shadow crossed her table.

"Well, well. What are you doing here?"

Ivy looked up to see her sister Shelly standing beside her table, sunglasses pushed over her windblown hair, a shopping bag dangling from her wrist. "I could ask the same of you."

"Java Beach isn't good enough for you anymore?" Shelly slid into the chair across from Ivy without waiting for an invitation. "The gang's all there working on the Bookfest plan. I just left."

Ivy closed her notebook. "I figured you, Poppy, and Libby had it under control. I needed a quiet space to make a few calls. How's it going on the project?"

"It's going to be fabulous," Shelly said, her enthusiasm

bubbling over as she set her shopping bag down. "We've already got half the town involved. Libby is amazing. She has authors lined up, and Poppy is working her event-planning magic. She constructed a master spreadsheet. It's going to come together very quickly."

"That's great. What have you done with Daisy?"

"Darla stole her," Shelly replied. "Brought a stroller and is parading her around town to all her friends. Just like a true grandma. I took advantage of the break to run some errands and was heading back when I spotted you. Since when do you hang out here by yourself, looking mysterious behind your dark sunglasses?"

Ivy lowered her sunshades. "Like I said, I needed to make some phone calls."

"About what?" Shelly leaned forward, her eyes narrowing with interest.

"I'm trying to find out if there might be a dormant bank account in Switzerland and how to pursue it."

Shelly's eyebrows shot up. "Do you think we could?"

"I've been researching, and there are still unclaimed accounts from the war years. The question is how to go about claiming one. We can't show up waving an old piece of paper."

Shelly rubbed her hands together. "This sounds like something out of a movie. Numbered accounts and all that. Do you really think there might be something there?"

"Maybe. If that's a bank account number, and if it still exists. And if it's in one of the Erickson's names."

Shelly stared at her for a moment. "Look, I'm the first to think about the money, but in this case, it was so long ago." Shaking her head, she reached across the table and squeezed Ivy's hand. "I can't believe money just hangs out somewhere without anyone noticing. I don't want to see you disappointed if this treasure hunt hits a dead end."

The concern in Shelly's eyes caught Ivy off guard, despite how much they'd been through together. "I know the odds, but I need to try. For Summer Beach and the library everyone deserves."

"Don't forget the art museum," Shelly added. "That's your dream, but you've hardly mentioned it."

Maybe because that seems so personal, Ivy thought. She'd love to curate a small collection. "That, too, of course."

Shelly studied her for a moment, then nodded. "So who are you going to call?"

"I already talked to Raquel in Mallorca," Ivy replied. "And I tried to reach Lea Martin, but I'm not sure if she's in London or Germany with her new husband. I left a message, so maybe she'll call me back."

"Okay, who's next?" Shelly asked.

"Viola, in San Francisco. She might have some advice."

Shelly waved to Hallie, motioning for another cup for coffee. "Make your call. I'll stay to give you moral support."

Ivy started to shoo her away but stopped. If they managed to recover funds for the library, it would be Shelly's win as much as hers. She'd stuck by Ivy since the beginning.

Since childhood, in fact.

"Okay. Here goes." Ivy tapped Viola's number on her phone and put it on speaker. After several rings, a distinct, formal male voice answered.

"Good morning. Standish residence. Who's calling, please?"

Ivy recognized the houseman's voice. "Hello, Leon. This is Ivy Bay from Summer Beach calling for Mrs. Standish."

"Yes, of course," Leon replied with warmth in his voice.

"How nice to hear from you. One moment, I will see if Madam is available."

"Must be nice," Shelly whispered.

Ivy put a finger to her lips. "Shh."

After a long moment, Viola came on the phone. "Ivy, darling. How lovely to hear from you. It's been too long, my dear. How is the renovation proceeding?"

"Very well. Thanks to you and your generous friends, the new Seabreeze Inn will be a centerpiece of the community. The construction crew is jack-hammering the driveway as we speak. I hope you'll come for the grand reopening."

"I wouldn't miss it," Viola said. "Amelia Erickson would be so pleased with what you've done with the place." She paused. "I know Gustav is, or so he professes."

Ivy could hear Meredith in the background scolding her. "Aunt Viola, people will think you're losing your mind if you keep talking about spirits."

Viola laughed. "Why, that's the fun of it. Everyone needs a little eccentricity to be interesting. Say hello to Ivy, darling."

The phone shuffled between them with sounds of buttons inadvertently pressed. "I think it's on speaker now," Viola said loudly. "Can you hear me?"

"We hear you," Ivy said, and Shelly chimed in. They traded pleasantries before Viola asked, "Now that you're tearing apart the old beach house, have you discovered anything else hidden there?"

Ivy grinned at Shelly. "That's why I'm calling. We made a discovery recently that's quite puzzling." She explained the architectural plans and the possibility of funds on reserve in a dormant bank account.

"I did some investigating," Ivy continued, her words spilling out. "I learned there are still unclaimed Swiss bank accounts dating from World War II. Even before. Do you or your attorney know if the Erickson estate had any such accounts?"

Viola was quiet for a moment, and Ivy's heart sank. Then the older woman spoke slowly, as if choosing her words carefully.

"We wouldn't have been privy to that financial information, my dear. Only as it related to the purchase of the house." She paused. "That said, I know of a fabulous young attorney who works for a firm that deals in such matters. The firm has helped families locate lost property from that era. Quite remarkable work."

Ivy's pulse quickened.

Meredith spoke up. "Aunt Viola is referring to my son Andrew. He works for a law firm in Los Angeles. Recently, he has been assisting clients who are Holocaust survivors and descendants. His team managed to recover bank accounts and artwork stolen many years ago. Swiss banks have very specific procedures. He'll know what to do."

"That's impressive." Ivy raised her brow at Shelly.

Meredith said, "I'll put you in touch with him. Expect a call soon."

"That would be incredible, Meredith. Thank you." Ivy's voice tremored with gratitude.

"Our pleasure, dear," Viola said. "Do keep us posted. How wonderful it would be to see Amelia's dream for a library and art museum come true."

After they hung up, Shelly burst into a grin. "Viola came through again. You got this."

Ivy shook her head as that strange panic set in again. "Not yet."

Instead of celebrating a premature win, she considered how all this sounded. *Money stashed away for decades simply falling into her lap.* This was more than a mere slim chance; this bordered on delusional.

Suddenly, she felt more than self-conscious. She felt ashamed. And she prided herself on being practical, except when pushed to desperation, like when she moved into the old beach house.

Shelly stared at her. "What's wrong with you? A minute ago—"

Ivy cut her off. "It's probably nothing more than an old note about an account long closed."

Shelly's expression fell. "Just when I thought you had finally embraced the outrageous."

Ivy's seagull landed on the railing again, much closer this time, and blinked at her. As it did, a strange sensation rippled through her. She leaned forward, speaking to it. "Maybe you are the spirit of an old mariner, or in this case, a fervent art collector."

Shelly wrinkled her brow in concern. "You're talking to birds now?"

Rubbing the back of her neck, Ivy grinned at her, giving in to her sister's optimism. "Okay, who cares if we're delusional?"

"That's right," Shelly said, brightening. "At least we're having fun."

Laughing, Ivy rose from the table. "Let's go check on the Bookfest progress."

As it turned out, Libby had left to work on her proposal for the city council, and Poppy returned to the inn. Reed's crew finished the demolition, so the noise level ratcheted down a few notches.

The paper covering the floors crinkled as Ivy walked

through, and the air was thick with the smell of dust and old wood. All around she could see evidence of progress.

Outside, she spied Poppy working on her laptop on the patio by the pool. She looked up when Ivy and Shelly neared.

"I hear the plans for the book festival are going well," Ivy said. Patrons at Java Beach had eavesdropped, and word was already spreading.

Poppy's eyes shimmered with happiness. "People are excited to get involved. Louise at the Laundry Basket said she's having reading withdrawals since the library closed. She volunteered to manage the bake sale."

"How kind of her," Ivy said, looking over Poppy's shoulder at the spreadsheet on her computer. She tapped an entry on the list. "For food trucks, call Marina at the Coral Cafe."

"Will do," Poppy said, adding to the list.

Ivy's phone rang, and she brought it from her pocket to answer it. "Hello?"

A young man spoke, "This is Andrew Fields calling for Ivy Bay."

"This is Ivy. Thanks for calling."

"I'm in the car," he said, sounding like he was on a speakerphone. "I'll be brief. I understand you spoke to Viola and my mother. I'm driving back from a client meeting in San Diego, so I could meet you in Summer Beach on the way. The highway exit is coming up. I realize this is short notice, but would that work for you?"

"Of course, if you don't mind meeting in a construction zone. We'll be here."

Ivy hung up, her faith in the impossible restored. "Andrew Fields will be here shortly. Let's get the plans and that document."

They filled in Poppy while they got ready to meet Andrew. "You work fast, Aunt Ivy."

"This is only a preliminary talk." Ivy didn't want to raise hopes, even though Shelly could hardly contain her enthusiasm.

When Andrew arrived, Ivy met him in the foyer and led him to the patio where they sat by the pool. He was younger than she'd expected, probably Poppy's age or a couple of years older. He had sandy hair, a lean physique, and eyes that held a serious expression. Overall, she had a positive impression of him, hardly surprising given who his mother and aunt were.

"This is quite the house," Andrew said, taking it in. "Aunt Viola is a real history buff, and she's told me about this place. I'm sorry I couldn't make the gala. My work often requires overseas travel."

"Viola was instrumental in driving the restoration." Ivy introduced him to Shelly and Poppy. "My sister and my niece, who also manage the inn."

"Nice meeting you," Andrew said, his gaze resting on Poppy for a moment longer than necessary. He turned back to Ivy. "May I see what you told Viola about?"

Looking at him with a smile, Poppy unrolled the plans. "We found these plans hidden behind a wall. That's not unusual around here."

Andrew nodded. "My mother shared the backstory."

"We also found this." Ivy placed the two parts of the paper on the patio table. "We wondered if this might point toward a dormant, unclaimed account."

He peered at the faded fountain pen script. "Those numbers could very well pertain to an account. Have you looked up this address?"

"It's a bank in Switzerland," Ivy replied.

Andrew read the notation. "'Funds on deposit for the Summer Beach Library and Art Museum.' That's interesting, and it might have applied at one time. Is this all you have to go on?"

Ivy's heart sank. This is what she feared, and she felt a little foolish. "All we've found so far. It's not enough, is it?"

"We've worked with less," Andrew replied. "It's entirely plausible, but I want you to understand there may be difficulties."

Still, Ivy asked, "Could you look into it?" She paused, biting her lip. "I'm sure your law firm is excellent, but I don't have much money to put toward this."

Andrew lifted a corner of his mouth. "Aunt Viola loves a good mystery, and since she put me through law school, I'm in no position to decline her wishes. This one's on her. I can't imagine it will take long. Do you have any documents that might establish ownership or heirs, such as a will, trust, or death certificate? Even old letters. Anything that might demonstrate intent."

Ivy's heart dropped again. "I'll scan and email what I can find."

Poppy spoke up. "I'll do that for you, Aunt Ivy." Her cheeks were flushed with excitement.

A smile lifted Andrew's lips, and he held Poppy's gaze with interest. "Here's my card. I look forward to hearing from you, Poppy."

Ivy started to thank him when a voice sounded behind them.

Reed had just returned. "Who's this?"

Turning to her nephew, Ivy introduced them and explained, "Andrew promised to help us investigate what we found."

Reed was pleasant enough, but Ivy detected an undercurrent between him and his sister.

"I should be on my way to beat the traffic," Andrew said.

"I'll be in touch, and I'll see myself out. I enjoyed meeting all of you."

Poppy stared after him until Reed waved a hand in front of her face. "Hey, you're not interested in him, are you?"

Flipping her silky hair back, she shrugged off his question. "You have no right to comment."

Reed ran a hand over his jaw. "Neither do you, but that didn't stop you."

"Actually, I've changed my mind about Libby," Poppy said. "We're working together on the book festival."

Reed folded his arms. "Does this mean you're giving me your blessing to see her? Not that I need it, you know."

Ivy and Shelly looked at each other and burst out laughing.

"What's wrong with you two?" Poppy asked, her face growing even more flushed.

Still chuckling, Shelly said, "You guys argue just like we used to with your dad and uncle. They never approved of anyone we liked."

Ivy nudged her. "They were usually right, though. As for them, well, thank goodness Forrest found your mom." Angela was a good match for their brother, Ivy thought. With five children of their own, their family was as rambunctious as the one she and Shelly had grown up in. Not that she would have wanted it any other way.

"Don't you have work to do?" Poppy said to her brother.

"I just wanted to meet the guy you were making googly eyes at," Reed said over his shoulder. "See you later."

Poppy blew out a breath. "Sometimes Reed drives me nuts."

"Andrew seems interesting," Ivy said, smiling at her niece. The last boyfriend hadn't turned out well for her. Still, Poppy was young and should be dating to discover what she liked. "I'll try to get some documents for you to send him."

That would be a copy of the trust, Ivy decided. Bennett had one in his files. She didn't have anything else. Technically, she had no claim on any funds.

If there was an account, would funds go to the trust to be directed to Amelia's designated charities?

Ivy had another idea. She had no claim, but Lea might. She shivered at the thought and checked her phone again. By now, it was nighttime in Europe. She let out a small sigh. Maybe she'd hear from Lea tomorrow. That would be another conversation.

Though she tried to temper her thoughts, Ivy's mind still sprinted ahead, vacillating between possibilities and the sheer absurdity of her expectation. And yet, after all these years, what if funds meant for a library and art museum still existed in the bank?

What if Amelia's dream, and her own, could finally be realized?

Even as she tried to temper her feelings, her pulse pounded. For the first time, the sound of hammers and drills didn't bother her because beneath the noise and chaos, there was hope.

"*A*nother fine date night," Bennett said, helping Ivy slip into her lightweight jacket.

She kissed him on the cheek. "Thank you, darling." His skin was warm from the cozy evening they'd spent in front of the fireplace at the Oceanview Cafe. His eyes reflected the renewed warmth they shared.

She had been married long enough before to know that every relationship had its share of challenges. But the difference between Bennett and her former husband, Jeremy, was profound.

Bennett was more than her husband, more than her lover; he was her best friend.

Tonight, they'd had a good conversation about Ivy's latest findings, though it wasn't over yet.

She adjusted a scarf her mother had given her as they started for the door. After sunset, spring evenings were still cool at the beach.

Before they left the restaurant, Bennett paused to talk to

Hallie. "That dark chocolate and orange mousse was delicious."

Hallie beamed. "I'm glad you enjoyed it. That's one of our specialties."

Her husband appeared from the kitchen, still in his chef's jacket. The two had met at the *Cordon Bleu* in Paris and worked at the Four Seasons Hotel in Houston before moving here for a quieter life.

"Everything was incredible," Bennett added.

He rested his fingertips lightly at the small of Ivy's back. Not in a possessive way but reassuring and respectful. It was a subtle, intimate gesture she enjoyed.

"We'll definitely return soon," she said.

As they stepped outside, the cool ocean air carried the sound of jazz music from Spirits & Vine. With most shops closed, the village streets were quiet except for the restaurants.

"Want to take the beach path home?" Bennett asked, his voice low.

Ivy nodded. The inn had become their home. Although her husband still owned his ridgetop home, it was currently leased out. The small chauffeur's apartment at the inn was their cozy home. They both liked the bustle and variety of people.

On the way, they strolled past Nailed It, where Jen was flipping the sign to *Closed* while George counted the register.

"Perfect timing," Jen called out. "Another five minutes and you'd have missed us completely."

"Late night?" Ivy asked.

"Lots of new building projects," George said. "New decks, barbecues, patio furnishings. If customers are here, we stay late."

Bennett laughed. "The price of success. See you around."

As they continued walking, Ivy spotted Megan and Josh

approaching from the direction of Spirits & Vine. The documentary filmmakers were deep in conversation but brightened when they saw Ivy and Bennett.

Megan waved them down. "How's the renovation going?"

"We've found some old architectural plans for a library and art museum," Ivy replied. "I might have some new material for your documentary soon." Megan had been investigating and writing a screenplay about Amelia Erickson.

Megan shook her head. "This documentary is turning into a never-ending story. Whenever I think we're close to finishing, you find something else to add. Not that I'm complaining; that only improves it. Call me when you have the full story, will you?"

Ivy promised. They said their goodnights and turned toward the deserted beach path. Ivy slipped off her shoes, and Bennett did the same. The sand was cool beneath her feet. She tucked her arm through Bennett's.

"You were starting to tell me about Viola's nephew," Bennett said, returning to their dinner conversation.

"His name is Andrew," she said, adding details about his experience on other cases Viola had mentioned. "He thinks my hunch about it being a bank account might be correct."

Bennett raised an eyebrow. "That's incredible."

"But he's asked for any documents we might have to prove intent. If funds are still there, and if we can prove intent, the city could be the beneficiary."

"Those are some big *ifs*. Do you have time to devote to this?"

"If there's even a small possibility of success, I should pursue it. I tried to call Lea to see if she might have some documents." However, since her mother died so young, Lea grew up in another family. Ivy knew much of her original family history had been lost.

Bennett took her hand. "I'll give you the documents I have from the trust. That was part of the discovery in the lawsuit Jeremy filed to tear down the beach house, so you have access to them."

"I only wish…" Ivy stopped, another idea forming in her mind. "Libby is a research librarian. Before she arrived here, she came across an old article about Amelia and her plan to build the library and art museum. I wonder if she could find more?"

Bennett studied her. "That's quite a coincidence."

"She latched onto the idea. That was part of what brought her here."

"Is it, though?" he continued, gazing at her thoughtfully. "Watching you, I no longer consider synchronicities mere coincidences."

Ivy gestured toward the moonlight spilling onto the ocean. "Maybe it's divine guidance, or the universe shifting the puzzle pieces back into their proper position."

"All I know is, we need to listen to our gut instincts more. And mine are telling me to do this…" He cradled her face in his hands.

She lifted her face to his for a kiss, shivering at his touch.

The tide rushed in, swirling around their ankles, nearly knocking them off balance. She cried out and clung to him.

"I've got you," he said, chuckling. He lifted her easily onto dry sand. "Can't let anything happen to you until you figure out this latest discovery."

"I hope you're right about instincts," she said, clasping his hand. "Because mine are screaming. I've got to follow this trail of clues."

.   .   .

172 | JAN MORAN

THE CROWD WAS BUZZING at Java Beach. Ivy cut through the throngs, nodding to Darla and Charlie, a local retiree who took small bets on all sorts of things, including whether she and Bennett would marry. She smiled to herself. She never knew who won or lost that bet, but she and Bennett were clearly among the winners.

She slid into the seat across from Libby, who was already nursing a chai latte. She wore one of her usual cotton sundresses with cowboy boots.

"Thanks for meeting me," Ivy began. Hardly able to sleep last night, she had sent Libby a message early this morning to see if she might find other press clippings related to Amelia Erickson and her project. "How is your bookmobile proposal going?"

"Almost finished," Libby said. "I've been working with Poppy and Shelly on the book festival plan, too." She hesitated. "About your message... I have a lot of information for you."

"So quickly?"

Libby fidgeted with her cup. "I didn't want to look like I had an obsession, but maybe I did. When I saw Shelly's first videos about the inn, I was hooked. I was drawn to Amelia Erickson's story and felt like I had a stake in the outcome, too. Does that sound weird?"

"Nothing sounds strange to me anymore."

Libby scrolled through her phone. "Want to see some of what I found?"

"Sure." Ivy hadn't expected results so quickly. She wondered if anything would be helpful.

"I took photos of every article I found and saved the links. It was like an ongoing story I couldn't get enough of." Libby tapped the screen. "Start here."

Ivy scanned through articles from *The San Francisco Chronicle*, the *San Francisco Examiner*, and the *San Diego Evening Tribune*.

Libby cleared her throat. "If it's intent you're looking for, Mrs. Erickson stated her intent often. Keep going."

At the next document, Ivy opened her mouth in surprise. "Minutes from City Council meetings at Summer Beach?" She glanced at the date. "This was right after the city was incorporated." The list continued, but Ivy had seen what she thought was enough. "Will you email that to Poppy?"

Libby tapped her screen. "Done. Will this research really help?"

"I hope so. You might have just secured yourself a library, Libby."

Still, Ivy knew it wasn't going to be that easy. Andrew had requested more crucial pieces of information.

After leaving Libby, Ivy put another call through to Lea. Once again, the call went straight to voice mail. She left another message and added, "I hope you're okay."

Ivy prayed nothing had happened to her, though for Lea's sake, not hers.

21

*T*he airy, mid-century modern City Hall was perched on a cliff, commanding sweeping views of the village and ocean beyond. Its expansive windows framed the coastal scene like a postcard. Ivy stood beside Libby at the reception desk, where Nan greeted them with professional warmth.

"Hello, ladies," Nan said, glancing up. "Here for the council meeting?"

Ivy introduced Libby. "Her bookmobile proposal is on the agenda tonight."

"Good luck, dear. I'll be pulling for you," Nan added in a whisper.

Libby's eyes flicked to a large banner that read, *Life is Better in Summer Beach*. "I sure hope that's true." She drew a deep breath and straightened her long skirt. "I'm nervous about appearing before the council."

Ivy touched her arm lightly. "Summer Beach and its people have been good to me. Not that I didn't love where I lived before. Boston was a wonderful city." She paused, choosing her words carefully. "But I had memories that were better left behind." When she saw surprise and curiosity on Libby's face, she said, "I'll tell you about it someday, but what's important is I found my purpose here. I have a feeling you will, too. You'll do fine, and many people are here to support you."

The sincerity in her voice seemed to steady Libby, whose shoulders relaxed a little. "I hope so. No one has ever said that to me."

The younger woman's words nicked Ivy's heart. How many people simply needed a kind word of encouragement to start on a path and fulfill their potential?

She smiled. "I've got your back, Libby. Will Reed be here?"

"He'd planned on it but got a call before I left. He said he needs to stay at the inn because his boss is coming by for an inspection."

That would be Forrest, Ivy knew. Reed's father was a stickler for proper procedures.

They entered the council chambers, where Bennett and the other council members were chatting and taking their seats. Ivy had made several proposals here since she'd arrived. Although the ocean view made official business feel less intimidating, the matters at hand were still important.

Ivy noticed how many friends and family members filled the audience seats. Shelly and Mitch sat near the front, with Poppy just behind them. Jen and George from the hardware shop waved from their seats, while the bookshop proprietor Paige thumbed through what appeared to be notes. Even Hallie from the cafe hurried in.

"Look at all this support," Ivy whispered to Libby, guiding her toward two empty seats.

Just then, a casually elegant woman with long, straight black hair flowing around her shoulders approached them.

"Libby, this is Celia and her husband, Tyler," Ivy said.

"They support local music classes and other educational programs in the Summer Beach schools." The young couple had retired to Summer Beach a few years ago.

Celia extended her hand. "We've heard about your book-mobile. It's what this community needs, at least until we find a permanent solution."

Tyler nodded. "We used to work in technology. Your proposal should pass, and we'd like to contribute funds for books. All kinds, but especially those about science and technology. Maybe you could engage with the subject on a fun level. The kids miss having a library outside of their school facility."

"Don't forget music and the arts," Celia said to Tyler.

Libby's eyes widened. "That's incredibly generous, thank you."

After the pair sat down, Ivy whispered to Libby, "You have a lot of support."

"I'm beginning to realize that." Libby's voice held a note of wonder.

Once the council members were seated, Bennett smacked his gavel and brought the room to order.

Ivy watched her husband, noting how he reviewed each item of business that came before them. He spoke with thoughtfulness rather than performative importance. When she caught his eye, he acknowledged her with only a slight nod. She appreciated that he never compromised his integrity. People respected him for that.

Those qualities had drawn her to him, and she still found them wildly attractive, though infuriating at times, such as with her requests.

Love could be complicated.

Three agenda items passed before Bennett called for Libby.

"Our final item of business is a proposal for a bookmobile contract."

As Libby walked to the front, Ivy noticed her hands trembling slightly, but her posture was straight and her gaze direct.

"Good evening, council members," she began in a quiet voice.

With a subtle gesture, Ivy touched her ear, encouraging her to speak up.

Libby increased the volume. "I understand that Summer Beach has been without library services since the closure of its library. The absence has left a gap in your community's services to all residents."

Ivy nodded her approval. The professional librarian in Libby was taking over.

She outlined her proposal with increasing confidence. She spoke of how her bookmobile would visit neighborhoods on a rotating schedule to bring books, internet access, and programming to all sections of Summer Beach.

"I've compiled data showing that communities with mobile library services see improved literacy rates and community engagement." She paused to distribute folders to the council members.

Bennett flipped through the material with a thoughtful expression. "This is impressive research. Have you worked with mobile libraries before?"

"Yes, Mayor Dylan. Before arriving in Summer Beach, I was employed as a research librarian and an outreach coordinator, managing a bookmobile that served surrounding rural neighborhoods."

Ivy felt a flutter of pride. Libby hadn't mentioned this experience to her.

A councilwoman with bold black glasses frowned. "The

proposal looks interesting, but where would new books come from?"

"I'm accepting donations to cover the cost. In fact, some here have already pledged support for new books. I'm also helping the Seabreeze Inn managers organize an annual book festival. The goal is to raise funds for books to augment my existing collection and eventually become part of a library collection."

One councilman shook his head with exasperation. "We have already addressed the library request. The city doesn't have the budget. Now or in the future."

"May I comment?" Ivy raised her hand, feeling the weight of every gaze in the room.

After Bennett recognized her, she stood and squared her shoulders. "Members of the community are making alternate arrangements to provide a library for Summer Beach residents. The bookmobile is an important interim measure because it might take us a while. But know that we are working on it, no matter how long it takes. Summer Beach will have another library, even if it is a privately supported facility."

Shaking his head, the last councilman leaned forward again. "A private library? Sounds a little far-fetched to me. Is that even a thing?"

"Actually, I'm very familiar with private libraries," Libby said. "I interned at the Huntington Library in Pasadena. It's known for its extensive research collection. It even has the papers of Presidents George Washington and Thomas Jefferson. So yes, private libraries are *a thing*. A very good thing."

A murmur rippled through the audience, followed by spontaneous applause. Ivy glanced at Bennett, whose expression remained neutral, but she caught the flicker of impressed surprise in his eyes.

After the applause subsided, the council members

conferred in low voices. Bennett leaned forward, speaking quietly to his colleagues. Ivy couldn't hear his words, but his body language conveyed support. They held a quick vote.

Bennett turned back to those in attendance. "After consideration, the council approves the bookmobile contract as proposed, with quarterly performance reviews." He swung his gavel again to adjourn the meeting.

Instant joy transformed Libby's face. When she returned to Ivy's side, she squeezed her hand. "I can't believe it," Libby said, her voice thick with emotion.

Ivy smiled and hugged her. "Better than the job in Los Angeles, right?"

"So much better," Libby said, laughing at the tale she had told.

Shelly threw her arms around her. "Way to go. You're one of us now."

"This is just the beginning," Ivy said, pleased at the growing support in the community.

Bennett joined them. He leaned in, whispering to Ivy. "How about another date night?"

"I have to meet Forrest and Reed at the house," she replied. "My brother is doing a walk-through."

"Mind if I join you?"

"I never mind. Let's go."

They left Libby to bask in the glow of her bookmobile victory, surrounded by Poppy, Shelly, and plenty of new supporters.

BENNETT FELL into an easy pace beside Ivy, catching her hand in his. "I'm curious to see how the renovation is progressing."

"So am I," she said, clasping his hand. "Reed's been

sending photos, but they don't capture the whole trans-formation."

"Unlike you, who sees the potential in everything."

His compliment warmed her. "Libby surprised me, though. When she first arrived, I wasn't sure what to think, but she turned out to be a rock star."

"You followed your gut instinct."

"Something like that," Ivy said, thinking about the guiding spirit that was likely still in residence, if that were possible.

As they approached the inn, Reed emerged from the front entrance, clipboard in hand, his demeanor more professional than she was accustomed to seeing from her nephew. Beside him stood his father, an imposing, fit figure of a man. His keen eyes were already assessing the exterior work.

"Right on time," Reed called out. "Dad dropped by to inspect our progress." The slight tension in his voice revealed how much his father's approval still mattered.

Forrest stepped forward to hug Ivy. "Had a job site nearby. Thought I'd see how Reed is upholding the company's reputation." Though his words sounded critical, the pride in his eyes when he glanced at his son told a different story.

"Bennett, good to see you." Forrest extended his hand. "Especially outside of the building department meetings. It's been a while."

"Likewise," Bennett said. "The city council meeting today was interesting. Once again, Ivy challenged the city."

Forrest chuckled. "What now, Sis?"

"A library and art museum for Summer Beach," she said with pride. "And if you're lucky, you might get a shot at building it."

He turned to Reed. "From the old plans you mentioned?"

"That's right. Interesting, huh?" While his father nodded his approval, Reed glanced at his watch. "We'd better stay on schedule or Mom will kill you." He gestured toward the entrance.

Forrest grinned. "Can't be late tonight. Let's see what you've done here."

As they stepped inside, Ivy was struck by how different the space felt. Light streamed through new windows, casting patterns across the freshly sanded wooden floors.

Forrest turned to Ivy. "Are you happy with the new windows?"

"Thrilled," Ivy replied. "You were right to suggest those. I can already tell they're less drafty and more efficient. I wasn't aware we could replace the old windows with the historic designation."

She had planned to restore the old windows, but Forrest encouraged her to look at new options since the inn was a public place with high traffic. An exception was made for those reasons.

Her brother nodded. "These windows match the original design and are better for energy efficiency. Your guests will appreciate that. Winters by the sea can be cold, even here."

Reed pointed out items of interest as they walked. "We've completed all the major structural work. Electrical and plumbing are now updated to code, and we added improved insulation where we could. Heating and air conditioning systems have also been replaced."

"The bones are solid now." Forrest ran an experienced hand along a smooth wall. "Nice work."

Reed straightened at his father's approval. "Tomorrow, we continue refinishing the original hardwood floors. They were in fairly good condition, though we replaced a few boards."

"I can't even tell where," Bennett said.

"As it should be." Forrest nodded in agreement. "That's the

mark of a fine craftsman. They're getting harder to find, but we have a good team."

Ivy followed them through the house, envisioning how it would look when completed. "What about the fixtures we discussed?"

"I saved everything salvageable." Reed led them to a side room where he'd organized vintage hardware in labeled bins. "The crystal doorknobs from the upstairs bedrooms are intact, but we're missing some, and a few were damaged. The bathroom fixtures are another story. Most should be replaced."

"We budgeted for that," Ivy was immensely pleased and relieved at the progress.

Bennett picked up an ornate brass door plate, examining it. "Craftsmanship like this is rare now."

"I've found online sources for period-appropriate replacements," Ivy said. "There's an architectural salvage shop in San Diego that specializes in coastal properties from this era. I want to honor the building's history while making it functional for today. That might go for the new library someday, too."

Bennett put his arm around her. "I like how you think."

As they continued through the house, Ivy noticed Bennett taking mental notes, asking Reed and Forrest intelligent questions. With his background in real estate, Bennett had more than the average knowledge.

She appreciated having an interested partner.

Reed showed them the work they'd done in the kitchen, which brought everything up to code but kept the vintage look. When they stepped outside in the car court area, Reed looked up at their quarters above the garage. "We haven't touched this section yet."

Ivy and Bennett looked at each other. "That's because we hadn't planned on doing much," Bennett said. "We can manage most improvements ourselves."

Forrest put his hands on his hips. "As long as our crew is here, you might as well take advantage of it. This was included in the budget."

Ivy was pleasantly surprised. "If we ever move, we could add this unit to the inventory. I know we hadn't planned on it originally, but if we have the budget to do it now, we should."

They all climbed the stairs and went inside.

Reed gestured around the space. "New paint at a minimum. Might as well sand and refinish the floors, too."

"That tragic kitchen sink should go," Forrest said, chuckling. "We'll add that to the list. Cabinets, too. They didn't use the same quality here as in the main house."

"That's true, though I want to keep the vintage look and feel," Ivy said, leading them to the bathroom. "I have a lot of ideas about this space."

They spoke for a while, and finally, Forrest said. "You won't be sorry, but you'll have to find a place to stay for a while. Poppy is moving home for the rest of the renovation."

Bennett turned to Ivy. "My sister has a nice guest bedroom she offered earlier. Shall I call Kendra?"

"Let's take her up on it," Ivy replied.

Bennett grinned. "Dave and I can jam on the guitars, and we can teach Logan."

"Sounds like fun." Ivy enjoyed spending time with Kendra, too.

As they discussed finishes and timelines, Ivy's phone vibrated. Glancing down, she saw a missed call notification from Lea. Her stomach tightened with disappointment. How had she missed it? Then she realized the call had come in during the council meeting.

Bennett noticed her expression. "Everything okay?"

"I missed a call from Lea. I need to speak to her."

"Go ahead," Bennett said. "We'll finish here."

Ivy hesitated, torn between her responsibilities to the inn and her growing unease about Lea's situation.

"The house has stood for nearly a century," Bennett added. "It can wait another hour."

"Thanks for that." She squeezed his hand before hurrying toward a table by the pool, mentally composing what she would say.

She hoped Lea would pick up.

22

*O*utside by the pool, the fresh air was a welcome relief to Ivy after the dust and paint fumes inside. The lazy rippling water should have been relaxing, but she was on edge about this conversation she needed to have with Lea.

She pulled out her phone and dialed Lea's number, willing her to answer. However, once again, the call went to voicemail, asking her to leave a message.

"Lea, it's Ivy again. I'm sorry I missed your call. Please call me back when you get this. It's important." She paused, wondering how much to reveal. "It's about something else we found in the house."

After ending the call, she ran a hand through her hair in frustration.

Just as she was about to rejoin Bennett, Forrest, and Reed in the house, her phone rang. It was Andrew. Ivy's pulse quickened as she answered.

"Did I catch you at a good time?" His deep voice carried the thoughtful, professional precision of a well-educated man.

"As good as it gets. What's going on?"

"I've submitted the legal request to the Swiss bank." His tone held a hint of satisfaction. "Their in-house counsel verified the long-dormant account. It's in the name of Amelia Erickson."

Ivy caught her breath. "The account exists?" She paced along the edge of the pool, energy surging through her limbs.

"The account number you provided was a match. This is significant because these banks guard their clients' privacy ferociously. They wouldn't have confirmed this much information without the court's involvement. But I have experience with reluctant financial institutions," he added with a hint of amusement.

"What do you mean by that?"

"For example, one bank tried to get away with only paying out the original principal and withholding interest earned and compounded over decades. There are other issues, too."

Ivy had no idea it would be so difficult. She would have to thank Viola again.

Andrew went on, "Consider hurdle number one cleared, and that's good news. Next, we must prove Lea Martin is the rightful heir. Did you talk to her?"

Ivy allowed herself a moment of triumph before reality reasserted itself. "I'm still working on that."

"If she can't establish that, the bank will not release funds." He grew more serious. "This might be a lengthy process. At some point, I'll need to fly to Switzerland with Lea or secure a power of attorney from her."

Ivy hoped Lea would agree to that. "And after that?"

"The final step will be proving the funds were intended for the library and art museum." He paused. "Are you confident Lea will agree to that?"

Ivy watched a leaf drift across the pool's surface, carried by invisible currents. "I don't know," she admitted. "She mentioned she was trying to sell her company. I imagine she will do well when it does."

"A lot can happen to change people's circumstances," Andrew said. "Money has a way of altering promises and priorities."

The implication hung between them, unspoken but understood. What if Lea decided to keep the entire inheritance for herself? She had every right to it. While she had relinquished any claim to the inn, she could have fought for it.

"I understand. I'm doing everything I can to reach her."

"Keep me posted," Andrew said. "I'll continue preparing. And please be patient. Countries have different banking procedures. While I remain hopeful, I can't say what the bank or the court will ultimately decide."

After he hung up, Ivy remained by the pool, thinking about the situation. The existence of the account validated everything she'd suspected, but without Lea's cooperation, they were still adrift. She wanted this so much for the community.

One step at a time.

She turned toward the house, where light spilled from the windows. Inside, Bennett was gesturing with enthusiasm as he spoke with Reed and Forrest. The three men were enjoying each other's company.

She was grateful this renovation project was coming along well. If it wasn't for sheer serendipity, it might never have happened.

Yet, uncertainty still swirled around this latest secret the old house had given up. For whatever reason, Ivy couldn't rest until she helped the former owner realize her dream. In doing so, she hoped to realize hers, too.

23

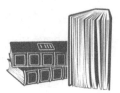

"That was a rare treat," Ivy said, leaning against Bennett. "I'm utterly stuffed."

They had just finished their take-out supper. The evening breeze rustled the palm trees surrounding their treehouse balcony where Ivy sat cross-legged on the outdoor sofa, sipping a cup of mango green tea. She loved this panoramic view of the beach.

"Relax with your tea," Bennett said, nuzzling her neck. "I'll do the dishes."

She laughed. "I like that trade. Be sure you scrub that pizza box well."

"It still counts, sweetheart." She could hear him chuckling as he walked back to the kitchen.

When her phone rang, she nearly knocked over her tea reaching for it. Seeing Lea's name on the screen sent a surge of relief through her. "I've been hoping to hear from you. Is everything okay?"

"Sorry for the delay in getting back to you," Lea replied,

sounding tired. "I've been in meetings all week about my company sale. It's been arduous."

"I can only imagine. Do you have a moment?"

"Barely, but I want to speak to you," Lea said. "I loved visiting Summer Beach and hope to return for a holiday. Viola also called and told me about some architectural plans for a library and art museum. It sounds like you need some documents from me. Her nephew is helping you, correct?"

"That's right." Ivy filled her in about the dormant funds, how they discovered the account, and that Lea was the heir.

Ivy closed her eyes, gathering courage. "I understand this is a big request, and you've already been so generous. Still, if you're confirmed as the heir, would you consider donating those funds to Summer Beach to build the library and art museum your great-aunt envisioned?"

The silence that followed stretched long enough that Ivy wondered if the call had dropped.

Finally, Lea spoke. "You're probably looking for a will and death certificate, yes?"

"Those would help establish your claim."

"And you need me to do that first."

Ivy pressed a hand to her heart. "That's right."

"Well then, you're in luck," Lea said. "I'll ask my attorney to express mail them to you tomorrow. It took me a long time to locate those documents, but I keep several official copies on hand now."

Ivy sat up, slightly shocked. "That would be incredible, thank you. Are you in London?"

"My husband and I are in New York, and we're finally celebrating the sale of my educational software company. I've been working toward this deal for the past year and signed the final papers this afternoon. This has been an enormous success, and I loved building the business, but I'm ready to start a new life with my husband now."

Ivy was genuinely pleased for her. "Congratulations. That's wonderful news."

Lea hesitated. "As for your situation, you should know that dormant account claims like this can take a very long time. These banks have held onto a lot of money for years, and it's not easy to assert rights to it for many reasons."

"I understand," Ivy said solemnly.

"However, if I am deemed the legal heir," Lea continued, "consider the funds yours. I might not have met my great-grandfather or Amelia, but I know they would be pleased to have an art museum in Summer Beach now. It's incredible to think she had plans drawn up. Art was their life, their common bond. I assume you're establishing a nonprofit entity to build and manage the library and art museum?"

"Andrew mentioned that," Ivy replied. "I appreciate your help. This will mean so much to Summer Beach residents."

"I'm glad you caught me," Lea said, sounding a little rushed. "We're leaving on a long trip soon. This first year of marriage has been so busy we've hardly had time to enjoy each other." Curiosity edged into her voice. "Where in town will this be built?"

"We're still working on that."

"Please keep me informed," Lea said. "I'd love to visit it. Even from beyond, Amelia Erickson has created such a lasting benefit for the place she loved. After all, that's what legacies are for, aren't they? To benefit those who come after us. Thank you for contacting me about this. All these years later, it will be a privilege to direct her funds where she wanted them if we are lucky enough to claim them. I sincerely hope this effort comes to fruition. If it does, I hope you will act as curator of the museum?"

"I've considered it, but that's a long way off. We have a lot to do before we reach that point." While the idea was appealing, Ivy wasn't sure how much time that would require.

After discussing the final details, thanking and congratulating Lea again, Ivy ended the call. Blinking back sudden tears of joy, she lowered the phone, overcome with Lea's generosity. It wasn't only about the money, Ivy knew.

Lea had once told her she'd been searching for a connection to the past to give meaning to her future. Her family had suffered during the war, and she had never known her parents or grandparents.

Ivy sat motionless for several minutes, watching darkness settle over the beach, studded with lights.

The possibility that had seemed so remote was now taking shape. Still, Ivy noted Lea's warning and remained cautiously optimistic. There were more challenges before her vision could become a reality.

For the first time since discovering the architectural plans, Ivy allowed herself to imagine walking through the completed library and the adjoining art museum.

Oh, what I could do with that, she thought. A student artist exhibit area, a section of female artists, or local California artists. There were plenty of talented people who hadn't received their full recognition.

This would be the first cultural center for the community.

She imagined sunlight streaming through windows, books lining shelves, art hanging on walls, and locals gathering in beautiful spaces designed nearly a century ago by a woman whose dreams had outlived her.

Maybe that was the nature of vision. To create what would outlast you, much like planting the proverbial tree whose shade you wouldn't live long enough to enjoy.

However, it all hinged on a foreign bank's acceptance of

decades-old documents. This project still needed community support, because she couldn't depend on that.

24

*I*vy stood watching the first annual Summer Beach
Bookfest at the old airfield, where she'd been setting
up since sunrise. The last few weeks had been a whirlwind of
activity. The book festival and the final construction phase on
the inn had kept Ivy's mind off the issue of the dormant bank
account that Andrew was working through. The Bookfest was
even more important to Summer Beach now.

"Nervous?" Bennett asked. He handed her a cup of coffee
from Mitch's Java Beach booth.

"Grateful," Ivy replied. "Look at all these people."

"They're here because of you," Bennett said. "Your vision
brought this entire event together."

Ivy dipped her head. "I wasn't the first to envision a library
for Summer Beach."

Bennett stared at her. "You called for a new library long
before you found those plans, and you rallied your team to
execute this event. Don't diminish your efforts."

"Did I just do that?" Ivy pressed a hand to her chest. "Oh,

my goodness, I did. Thanks for catching that. I warn Misty and Sunny about being too modest."

She shook her head, realizing she'd just fallen into the trap of automatically minimizing her efforts. Modesty was one thing, but downplaying accomplishments was quite another. Many women of her generation and those before still had society's old rules for women embedded in their subconscious minds.

And that was so last century.

Bennett put his arm across her shoulders. "You made this happen, sweetheart, despite lacking city council support."

"Maybe someone ought to start a recall campaign of that short-sighted mayor." Ivy grinned.

"I never want to come up against you in a popularity contest. You'd win, hands down."

Ivy laughed, teasing him. "Better watch your back then."

Raising her chin, she gazed over the throngs of book lovers with satisfaction. The old Seabreeze Shores Airfield was now a bustling hub of literary celebration.

Vendor tents and families populated the sunny expanse, but it hadn't always looked this way. During Prohibition in the 1920s, mobster Tony Diamond built the airfield to smuggle booze into the states and onto gambling barges anchored off the coast beyond the legal line. Recently, Ivy and her family had been part of the effort to repurpose the former runways as bike trails and walking paths.

Today, the turnout exceeded even Ivy's most optimistic projections. People lined up to pay a modest admission fee, and families spread blankets on grassy areas between booths where authors were signing books.

Bennett's sister Kendra and her family had brought blankets and chairs. She and Bennett were staying with them while Reed's crew was renovating their apartment, among the last of the units at the inn. Ivy was grateful to Bennett's family. Kendra and Dave had made them feel so comfortable and welcome.

Poppy was navigating the happy crowd, directing volunteers. She gathered Ivy, Bennett, and Libby together. "It's time to welcome everyone to the Bookfest."

When she gave the signal, Ivy picked up a microphone and said, "Good morning, book lovers." She waited a moment for the enthusiastic cheers to die down.

"Welcome to the inaugural Summer Beach Bookfest," Ivy began, her voice carrying across the gathering. "Thank you for coming and supporting efforts to bring a library back to Summer Beach. As many of you know, the Ericksons were early settlers and built what is now the Seabreeze Inn. If Mrs. Erickson were here today, I know she would be pleased to see how her dream of bringing books and art to our community inspires us nearly a century later."

She gestured to the colorful scene around them, where authors signed books, children explored Libby's bookmobile, and people mobbed the *Blind Date with a Book* table of exquisitely wrapped literary surprises.

"This festival represents more than just a fundraiser for our future library. It's about our community taking ownership of this effort." Ivy paused, taking in the familiar faces around her. "Building a library may take years. It will require persistence, creativity, and your continued support. But today is proof that Summer Beach values the written word, the exchange of ideas, and the creation of spaces where everyone belongs."

Applause rippled through the crowd, and she passed the microphone to Bennett, who added a few words about the city's support of the new bookmobile service and introduced the city's new librarian. Standing beside the mayor, Libby beamed.

After Bennett's talk, several townspeople approached him. Ivy knew he'd be busy, so she strolled through the festival, enjoying the excitement. She stopped to chat with authors, admired children's artwork inspired by favorite books, and helped an elderly couple find a shaded seating area.

"Hey, you," Shelly called to her. "Great welcome speech."

Ivy joined her in the children's tent. "I'm thrilled with the turnout."

Daisy sat in her sister's arms, entranced by a hand-puppet show about baby barnyard animals.

"This is incredible," Shelly said. "I've never seen her sit still for this long. Maybe I should whip up some sock puppets at home."

"That's easy to do. Kids often like simple toys the best. My girls loved playing with boxes and banging wooden spoons. Building a blanket fort was always popular."

"Hey, babes." Mitch appeared, balancing a tray of pastry samples from his Java Beach booth. He bent to kiss Shelly and Daisy on the cheeks.

Shelly grabbed a couple of cinnamon roll bites. "How's business?"

"Better than expected," he replied. "We'll probably sell out before we make it to the silent auction or readathon. You guys sure planned a full schedule. Have you been by the auction booth?"

Curious now, Ivy craned her neck, spying her beach paintings displayed in the silent auction tent. "Any interest yet?"

Mitch nodded. "People are bidding up your seascape. It should fetch a good price."

"How about your Java-for-a-Month donation?" Shelly asked.

"That one's hot, too." Mitch grinned at his joke. "See you all later."

After Mitch moved on, Daisy returned her attention to the puppet show.

"Have you heard from your attorney lately?" Shelly asked, lowering her voice.

Ivy frowned, knowing Andrew had hit a rough patch. The bank account claims process had slowed during the last few weeks due to legal issues. "He's in Zurich now on other business, so he will present the claim. We're still hoping the process moves forward."

"And if it doesn't?"

"Then we continue doing what we're doing right now," Ivy replied. "Raising funds and building community support. Eventually, we will build a stunning library and museum complex for the town."

"Look, Ives," Shelly whispered. "I know those are amazing plans, but have you thought about scaling back? We could build a smaller library sooner. After all, what does Summer Beach really need?"

Ivy stared at Shelly. "Are you starting to doubt this now?"

"It's just that you're usually the practical one, and I'm the woo-woo, let's-dream-it-big-and-they-will-come one."

"Maybe you're rubbing off on me."

Shelly shook her head with concern. "I don't know if that's a good thing."

"Look around you," Ivy said, gesturing. "People who might never have met are bonding through books. We don't need an old bank account payout to make this dream a reality. Between this and other sources, we can do it." She hoped her sister wouldn't ask what other sources she had in mind, because she didn't have any of the same magnitude.

Shelly blinked, taking this in. "You sound almost philosophical about potentially losing millions."

"I'm being realistic," Ivy said. "Even if Andrew produces a

positive outcome, a library needs an annual operating budget. The initial funding would be transformative, of course. Either way, we will need Bookfest for a long time."

Shelly nodded slowly. "Have you talked to Libby lately? She has so many ideas for the library. Like after-school programs, summer reading events, computer workshops, even a seed library that I volunteered to organize. People would love that."

"She also mentioned a backpack program for students who can't afford school supplies," Ivy added. "The library would be a central hub for community needs."

"And you're okay with waiting on those services just to build a larger building? Is this about serving the community or pointing to a huge building so you can say, 'I did that.'?"

Ivy wasn't sure where this was coming from, but she had to concede that Shelly had a point. "Well, that's an alternative to consider."

"Look, I just want Daisy and other kids to have a library before they grow up. Like we did. All I'm saying is, it's okay to compromise."

She rested her hand on Shelly's arm, acknowledging her insights. "I get it. Let's talk about this later."

Ivy chewed her lip as she walked back to the main staging area. Was this a vanity project for her? Maybe it was. Maybe she wanted to prove something.

But didn't they all?

She worried about disappointing everyone if the dormant account funds fell through. She had already asked those who knew about this not to mention the possibility until funds arrived in Summer Beach.

However, she also realized that might never be. They needed another plan, too.

Ahead, volunteers were setting up rows of chairs for the

readathon. Bennett was in conversation with an elderly man Ivy recognized as a retired professor from the community college.

Her husband was right, too. With or without a financial windfall, Summer Beach had to support its services.

Just then, her phone rang. It was Andrew. "Hello?"

"I'm sorry it took me so long to check in with you." Andrew sighed deeply. "I wanted to wait until I had good news to report."

Ivy clutched the phone, listening. However, a little voice in her mind had already told her all she needed to know.

Once again, she would have to start over.

25

*P*re-dawn pearl-gray moonlight shone through the new gauzy bedroom curtains when Ivy's phone erupted. Startled awake and disoriented, her heart raced.

Has something happened to Misty or Sunny?

Beside her, Bennett stirred, instinctively reaching for his phone in the half-light. "What time is it?" he murmured, his voice rough with sleep.

Ivy fumbled for her phone, squinting at the screen. "It's Andrew," she said, suddenly fully alert.

She tapped the phone with trembling fingers, putting the call on speaker at Bennett's gesture.

"Sorry for the early call, but I'm at the bank in Switzerland." Andrew's voice crackled a little on the line. "I'm here with Lea and her husband. Everything is proceeding, but we've hit a complication. We hope you can help."

Bennett sat up beside her, running a hand through his sleep-tousled hair.

"What kind of complication?" Ivy tried to keep the anxiety from her voice.

"There's a password on the account. The bank is requesting it before they'll release access. Do you have any idea what it might be? Maybe a word or phrase written on another piece of paper, or even on the plans."

Oddly, Ivy had a weird dream last night about this, probably from some research article she'd read. She closed her eyes, trying to put herself in Amelia's place. Or would it have been her father? She breathed out. No, he would use a password his daughter would remember.

What might Amelia use?

"It might be Gustav…"

"No, that's not it," Andrew said quickly.

Her eyes still closed, she pictured Amelia here. *Walking on the beach….* Words materialized in her half-awake consciousness. "Try Summer Beach."

There was a pause and a murmured conversation on the other end, then Andrew's voice returned. "I'm sorry, no luck."

She closed her eyes again, visualizing a beach scene. *Amelia turns toward her house, her heart full of love. She whispers…*

In a flash, she knew. "It's Las Brisas del Mar."

More voices floated through the phone line. Andrew came back on. "That's it." He lowered his voice. "How did you know?"

"That was the home's original name, before it became the Seabreeze Inn." Relief washed through her.

"We've cleared another hurdle. I'll call later with another progress report."

After they disconnected, Ivy rubbed her face, processing what happened.

"That was a good guess," Bennett said, taking her in his arms. "And from a dead sleep. I'm impressed."

"It wasn't a guess. It just came to me, as if I heard it." Ivy was slightly awed over the experience, too.

"Maybe you did," Bennett said, burying his face in her hair. "Come on, we won't get back to sleep now. Might as well start the coffee, unless you have another good idea." His eyes twinkled, teasing her.

Ivy wrapped her arms around his neck and kissed him. "I'll take you up on that later. But for now…" She whipped off the covers. "I'll race you to the kitchen. Dibs on the coffeemaker."

Bennett dove for her but missed. "Hey, it's my turn, you know."

They had just returned to their newly renovated quarters. The kitchen was updated with fine cabinets and countertops, while still maintaining many of the vintage elements. The tile was refurbished, walls painted, and a new retro-style refrigerator added.

The pride of their cozy kitchen was a fancy new espresso machine they'd splurged on.

Ivy added fresh coffee beans and turned it on. "Here it goes."

"Right behind you, sweetheart." He wrapped his arms around her, laughing.

A whirring noise filled the kitchen. Like a couple of kids, they watched the machine grind and brew the perfect espressos.

"This is the nectar of the gods," Ivy said, handing him a warm cup. The smell was intoxicating.

In the brisk morning air, they slipped into thick terry cloth robes and cuddled on the balcony. They talked about their day ahead while they watched the sun rise over the ridgetop. Ivy loved the quietness of simply being together.

Soon, they saw a light in Poppy's room in the cottage quarters, which were also finished now.

"That's our signal," Bennett said, rising from his seat. "I'll start breakfast."

The large kitchen in the main house was still under renovation. Reed had sent the twin vintage refrigerators and ovens out for refurbishment. When asked what color she wanted them, she'd told him, "Any color as long as it's turquoise."

Some things simply couldn't be improved upon. Bert and Bertie would live on in their kitchen.

Once they reopened for business, the usual rhythm of life would return. Laying out breakfast for guests, welcoming newcomers. Shelly teaching a yoga class while Ivy led the beach walk. Painting lessons by the sea. Just thinking about this eased her mind and lessened the panicky feelings she'd had.

But for now, life was just about family gathering in a sweet little kitchen.

"Do we have ripe avocados?" Bennett asked.

"Might be some in the basket on the table." Ivy drained her coffee. "I'll check them."

As they got breakfast underway, Bennett started the bacon and sliced avocados while Ivy whisked eggs and pureed green smoothies. The aroma of sizzling bacon filled the air just as Shelly arrived with a bag of fresh-picked oranges from the garden. Daisy was toddling beside her now.

Poppy followed them in, already looking bright-eyed.

"Wow, breakfast is early this morning," Shelly said. "Couldn't sleep?"

Ivy grinned. "Not since we got a call from Andrew in Switzerland."

"Any news?" Shelly asked.

Poppy hid a smile with her hand.

Noticing that gesture, Ivy realized she'd probably spoken to Andrew. Poppy had let slip that they'd been talking on the phone a lot. But he didn't share anything about the case with her due to client confidentiality. "Andrew called from the bank. He needed more information."

Shelly spread her hands in shock. "Wait, was this a good news call?"

"Maybe, but anything could still happen." Ivy slid an omelet onto a plate. "We need to prepare for either outcome."

"Always the pragmatist now," Bennett teased, but his eyes held admiration.

She smiled. "I've learned, painful as it was."

Bennett arranged avocado slices over the omelets and passed them around while Ivy poured the green drinks and Shelly peeled oranges.

Daisy tasted the smoothie Ivy had put in a sippy cup for her. She cooed her delight. "Mmm, good," she added in a sweet sing-song voice.

"One of her new words," Shelly said, smiling. "After mama, da, and no."

They settled around the small table, conversation flowing despite the underlying tension. Ivy updated them on the inn, Poppy reported the earnings from the Bookfest, and Shelly reported on the new spring plantings.

When Ivy's phone rang again, she leapt to answer it. Everyone's eyes fixed on her.

"It's Andrew," Ivy said, answering with speakerphone enabled. "We're all here. Bennett, Shelly, and Poppy, too."

"Then I have an audience for the good news." Andrew's voice lifted with pride. "It's official. It's been determined that Lea is the rightful heir. The account will be turned over to her."

Ivy was thrilled, yet despite her call with Lea, she was hesitant to make assumptions. "Please tell her congratulations."

"There's more," Andrew said. "She has also signed an agreement donating the funds to a nonprofit entity, The

Amelia Erickson Library and Museum, specifically for constructing and maintaining a permanent facility. It will be under your control, Ivy."

His words hung in the air, seeming almost unreal. Yet, it was, at long last. Ivy gripped the counter, nearly overcome with tearful relief. "Thank you, Andrew," she managed to say, her voice quavering with emotion. "And my deepest appreciation to Lea."

The kitchen erupted in celebration. Shelly cried, "Woohoo! That's what I'm talking about!" Little Daisy squealed with delight.

Bennett pulled Ivy into his arms. "Congratulations, my love."

Then, Shelly asked the big question. "What was the final figure? Will it be enough?"

There was a pause before Andrew answered. "The original deposit, plus close to nine decades of interest and investment returns, amounts to a very tidy sum."

When he gave the final tally, Ivy sat down abruptly, her legs suddenly unable to support her. The figure was beyond anything she had imagined.

Poppy stared at her, wide-eyed. "That's enough for the building and an endowment for operating costs."

"Exactly," Andrew confirmed. "Lea has specified that after the building costs, the principal shall remain untouched, with the annual returns funding operations in perpetuity. The building itself will be named The Amelia Erickson Library and Art Museum, with a special plaque in remembrance of her father, Hans."

When the call ended, Ivy sat in stunned silence, the reality of what they had accomplished sinking in.

"Here's to you, darling." Bennett raised his water glass to Ivy, and everyone around the table did the same.

"I can hardly believe it's over." Ivy was overcome with the magnitude of what had just happened. It was one thing to dream, and quite another to execute. "And now, it's the beginning of the project, isn't it?"

"What's next?" Poppy asked, looking excited.

Ivy pressed her fingertips against her temples in thought. "We'll have the architectural plans updated so Forrest can work up a favorable estimate for us. We'll organize the board and start making plans." She glanced out the window at the inn, which was looking quite elegant again. "Here we go again."

Shelly wiped Daisy's face. "You wouldn't be happy unless you had a challenge. You've always been that way."

"Then I must be ecstatic." Ivy laughed because her sister was right. "But someday, I'd like to have a little leisure time. Probably not for a long time, though."

Bennett kissed her cheek. "That's what vacations are for. "Maybe we should plan a long weekend getaway before the inn reopens."

"I'd love that." Ivy threw her arms around him. Bennett knew what she needed, sometimes more than she realized.

She'd kept her emotions tightly contained for a long time, but now, they burst free, whizzing through her like a wild roller-coaster.

"You're shivering," he said, rubbing her arms. "Probably from the adrenaline rush of all this."

Shelly eyed her sister. "Why don't you two go for a walk on the beach or take a ride? We'll clean up here. Go digest this, Ives. You really put your heart into this one."

Ivy turned to hug her sister. "Look at how far we've come. Thanks, Shells. You've always been a part of this, too." She sniffed back tears that sprang to her eyes. "And you, too, Poppy."

"Let's go, sweetheart." Bennett brought her favorite hoodie, and the two of them set off for the beach, leaving Shelly and Poppy, who were making lists of next steps.

"A library and art museum for Summer Beach hardly seems real," Ivy said, strolling beside him on the beach. "All that time searching, hoping, and piecing together fragments of Amelia's life. Now her dream will exist."

"Because you refused to give up," Bennett said, studying her. "Your determination inspired an entire community."

She dodged the icy water rushing onto the shore. "It wasn't just me. I like to think Amelia's spirit was somehow guiding me."

"You were the catalyst." He drew her close as they walked. "You saw possibility even before you discovered those plans."

Realizing what she was doing again, she paused, filling her lungs with air. "I did, didn't I?" Acknowledging her accomplishment felt surprisingly good.

Bennett nodded at that. "Have you ever thought maybe it wasn't a spirit leading you, but rather, you attracted the elements you needed?"

"Shelly once said something like that. I thought it was a little woo-woo, but she might have a point." Ivy looked up at the bright morning sky. "If that's true, I've had it backward. Is that what you mean?"

"Who's to say?" He smiled and caught her hand. "What I know is you're a resourceful, visionary woman. Look at what you've created here. A life that you wanted and deserved, that benefits everyone around you." Squeezing her hand, he added, "I'm sure glad it includes me."

"I don't think I'd want it any other way." She grinned and lifted her chin like a queen. "Not today, anyway."

"Hey, don't let your newfound power go to your head." He

swept her into his arms and whirled her around while she laughed with delight.

Ivy shook her hair back, smiling with happiness. With Bennett's arms around her, she felt more loved than ever—outside her family and daughters. Caring for her family and guests, gathering around a table with laughter, taking an impromptu walk on the beach with Bennett—these were the simple joys she loved in her life.

Her accomplishments over the past weeks filled her with satisfaction. At last, with the renovation nearly completed, she could turn her attention to a reopening party.

Bennett let her down, and her toes touched the sand. The cool breeze on her face brought a fresh thought to mind.

"We have twice as much to celebrate," she said. "The reopening of the inn and now, the kickoff of the library and art museum project."

"One project ends and another begins." Bennett swept fine strands of hair from her lashes and kissed her forehead. "About the library—it all worked out, didn't it?"

"As it was meant to, it seems." Ivy could hardly wait for the next chapter in their lives. She lifted her lips to his for the sweetest of kisses.

EPILOGUE

*T*he sun shone brightly on the empty lot off Main Street. Ivy stood at the edge of the gathered crowd, taking in a sea of familiar faces assembled for the groundbreaking ceremony. A buzz of anticipation filled the air. She looked around, pleased with the turnout.

Darla, Louise, and Paige had rallied the book clubs. Gilda toted Pixie in a pink doggie backpack while Imani and Clark chatted nearby with Jen and George.

Mitch's Java Beach patrons and Hallie and her husband from the Oceanview Café were there. Many others had arrived for the celebration, too. With encouragement from their teachers, children and their families poured in to celebrate the groundbreaking.

"Nervous?" Bennett asked, appearing at Ivy's side in a crisp white shirt and khakis that still made her look twice.

"Grateful for everything," she replied. Her ivory linen dress and colorful scarf fluttered in the ocean breeze.

People stood in line for her friend Marina's Coral Cafe food truck parked on the street for the event. Marina served refreshments and book-themed treats; the Mondrian-styled cake with bright color-blocked layers was popular. The red-and-white striped hat-shaped cookies inspired by Dr. Seuss's *Cat in the Hat* were also going fast, as were the artist palette-shaped cookies with colorful paint-like splotches.

He glanced at his watch. "It's almost time, but we should wait a little longer."

Today was almost perfect. "I wish the girls could—"

Suddenly, a commotion at the back of the gathering interrupted her, and Misty and Sunny raced toward her. "Mom!"

Beside her, Bennett laughed, looking relieved.

"What a wonderful surprise," Ivy said. She held out her arms to them, and they quickly enveloped her in a tangle of arms. "I didn't think you could make it."

"We wanted to surprise you earlier," Sunny said. "The traffic was heavy, but Bennett said he'd stall for us."

Misty grinned. "It's not every day your mother discovers a lost fortune and breaks ground on a new cultural center."

Her eldest daughter had been rehearsing for a new television pilot. Sunny had been busy with fieldwork for her course of study. They both looked happy, with a sprinkling of freckles across their noses the sunshine always brought out.

They spoke for a few minutes, and then a bell rang, signaling the start of the event. Poppy stepped up with a microphone for Bennett and switched it on. As mayor, he would introduce this new project to Summer Beach residents.

Ivy stood beside him, her heartbeat quickening with excitement.

"Welcome, friends," he began. "We stand today on this vacant lot. Some of you might think the city is behind this new project. But like many things in Summer Beach, appearances can be deceiving."

Laughter rippled through the audience.

"None of this would have been possible without Amelia Erickson's extraordinary gift that remained hidden for nearly a century," Bennett said. "That might have been lost forever if not for the tenacity and vision of one person who began lobbying the city for a library even before this discovery. Most of you know Ivy, my wonderful wife."

She smiled as applause rose in the air.

Bennett paused before going on. "Ivy connected threads nearly severed by time, refusing to let Amelia Erickson's vision fade into history. As a result, today we break ground on a new cultural center for the community."

Ivy felt a curious sensation, as if Amelia was watching from just beyond the visible crowd, finally witnessing her dream taking shape.

Bennett held his hand to Ivy, and the admiration in his eyes flooded her with emotion. She took the microphone from him and thanked him.

"I'm far from alone in this effort," she said, turning to Lea. "None of this would be possible without our dear friend Lea Martin, the great-niece of Amelia Erickson."

She gestured to Lea and her husband, who had recently arrived. Lea had made an additional donation to purchase this land, ensuring Amelia's vision would have the perfect spot in the center of town.

Lea inclined her head in acknowledgment.

"As it turns out," Ivy said, "the Gutierrez family purchased this land from the Erickson estate years ago. We've discovered this is the property the library and art museum had been designed for. That means we've come full circle to realize Amelia Erickson's original dream for the community. Please show Lea how much we appreciate this incredible gift."

Cheers and applause rang out, and Ivy touched her heart

in gratitude. She had been thrilled to discover that bit of history from Boz in the planning department.

Ivy went on to express her appreciation to those who had been instrumental in helping to secure Libby's bookmobile in the interim, including Celia and Tyler, who made a generous donation for new books, and Carol and Hal, who funded computers for the bookmobile.

Amidst more applause, Ivy's brother Forrest stepped up with a shiny ceremonial shovel festooned with a red bow. He handed it to Bennett, who said, "And now, the moment you've all been waiting for."

Poppy moved into position with her camera.

"Here goes," Ivy said, raising her voice. The crowd drew closer as she put her espadrille to the shovel. However, the dirt was so hard-packed she made only a slight indentation. She laughed at the absurdity of it. "Oh, my goodness. Looks like I need help with this groundbreaking ceremony."

Quickly, Bennett stepped up. "How about I take the other side?"

"That's good; hold that pose again," Poppy said, adjusting her camera against the sunshine. She snapped a few shots. "Since this new cultural center has been such a long time in the works, let's make sure we have good photos for posterity."

Forrest chuckled along with the rest of the family. "Don't worry about breaking up the dirt. We have heavy equipment for that."

"Dig, dig," Shelly called out, cheering them on as Misty and Sunny joined in. Mitch held Daisy on his shoulders, and Reed was standing with Libby. Andrew had also made a special trip from Los Angeles.

"I think we're making headway," Bennett said while Ivy laughed. They put their weight onto the shovel. Finally, the earth shifted.

"No wonder," Bennett said, scooping up a shovelful of dirt. "That looks like old concrete under there."

"On a vacant lot?" Ivy shook her head. "I didn't think anything ever existed on this property."

"Could be buried treasure," Shelly said, laughing.

"Hold it there," Poppy said, taking more photos.

"Wait, this isn't quite right." Ivy gestured to her niece. "Let's turn around to get everyone in the photos behind us. Because this library and art museum is for every person here."

Poppy turned and reframed the photo with the crowd surrounding them. "That looks much better. Hold up the sign, too."

Residents stretched the banner that read *The Amelia Erickson Library and Art Museum.*

"One more change," Andrew said, stepping to Poppy's side. "You should be in the photos, too. I'll take them."

Poppy's face brightened at his offer, and she took a spot beside Shelly. "Okay, on three, let's all wave our hands and say sea breeze." On her count, the crowd erupted in a roar of laughter.

After they finished the photos, Bennett returned the shovel to Forrest while Ivy chatted with her friends and neighbors.

"These cupcakes look yummy," Shelly said, returning with a cupcake that featured a gummy worm burrowed in the thick icing. Daisy reached for it, cooing with delight.

"What's that supposed to be?" Ivy asked.

Shelly pinched off a portion for Daisy. "It's from *The Very Hungry Caterpillar* book we read to Daisy. And the rest of this is for the very hungry mommy." She polished off the cupcake in a few bites.

As Ivy laughed, her daughters joined them. She was so happy they'd both made it today.

"I thought you might need something cool," Misty said,

handing her a bottle of water she'd brought from the food truck. "Marina's menu is so clever."

"She consulted with Libby on art and literary-inspired offerings," Ivy said.

The newest resident in Summer Beach was settling into the community and making friends. Libby and Reed were seeing quite a lot of each other now, and Ivy was happy for them.

"I brought an assortment of goodies for us." Sunny held up a plate of sweet treats, pointing to each one. "This is Bilbo's Lemon-Glazed Caraway Seed Cakes from *The Lord of the Rings*, Peach Cobbler from *James and the Giant Peach*, and Fruit Tarts from *Alice's Adventures in Wonderland*."

"Delicious," Ivy said, taking a tart and a miniature lemon bar decorated like a book. "It's so good to see you together again." Although she'd seen each of her daughters since New Year's, they hadn't returned at the same time.

Now, the inn was complete enough for them to stay in the guest rooms again this weekend. Once the final walk-through was signed off, the inn would open to the public with a grand reopening event.

As they were talking, Ivy overheard Andrew approach Poppy and ask her out for dinner for the evening. The smile that bloomed across Poppy's face was answer enough.

Bennett excused himself and crossed to her side, slipping an arm around her waist with easy affection.

"Happy?" he asked.

"Beyond words," she said, smiling at her daughters, who were circulating and enjoying themselves.

"They wanted to surprise you. I merely facilitated the conspiracy."

At that moment, with her daughters and family nearby and her husband and community around her, Ivy understood the richness of Summer Beach wasn't in buildings or bank accounts but in experiences that connected them. And soon, to every person who would walk through the library doors.

She leaned into Bennett and smiled. Some dreams were patient enough to wait for the right moment to bloom.

THANK you for reading *Seabreeze Library*, and I hope you enjoyed the excitement of bringing a new library to Summer Beach.

NEXT: Read *Seabreeze Harvest*, another heartwarming chapter in the beloved Summer Beach series.

BONUS! Discover more in Summer Beach. Download your free Summer Beach Welcome Kit now!

https://janmoran.com/SummerBeachWelcomeKit

SHOP: Keep up with my new releases on my website and online shop at JanMoran.com. You can shop exclusive ebook, paperback, and audiobook bundles ONLY on my bookshop at store.JanMoran.com.

JOIN: Please join my VIP Reader's Club to receive news about special deals and new releases. Plus, find more fun and join other like-minded readers in my Facebook Reader's Group.

MORE: Want more beach fun? Check out my popular Coral Cottage and Crown Island series and meet the boisterous, fun-loving Moore-Delavie and Raines families, who are always up to something.

Looking for sunshine and international travel? Meet a group of friends in a series all about sunshine, style, and second chances, beginning with Flawless and an exciting trip to Paris.

Finally, I invite you to read my immersive family sagas, including *Hepburn's Necklace* and *The Chocolatier*, 1950s novels set in gorgeous Italy.

Most of my books are available in ebook, paperback, hardcover, audiobook, and large print. And as always, I wish you happy reading!

SEA BREEZE COCKTAIL RECIPE

One of my most requested recipes is one that my friend Aly from New Zealand often whips up in honor of blazing sunsets over the Pacific Ocean. In fact, this recipe inspired the name of the *Seabreeze Inn* novel, and in the series, sisters Ivy and Shelly Bay are often found mixing Sea Breeze coolers — virgin or fully loaded, as we say. Whichever your preference, these yummy, colorful juice cocktails or mocktails are a treat on warm days. Cheers!

Just in case you can't read the image above, here are the recipes from *Seabreeze Inn*:

Compliments of Ivy and Shelly Bay

Sea Breeze and Bay Breeze Coolers are refreshing tonics that conjure beachside sunsets. These fruit juice blends are just as yummy without alcohol, too. Adjust the ratios of juices for taste as desired.

SEA BREEZE COOLER

4 oz. cranberry juice drink
1 oz. ruby red grapefruit juice drink
1 oz. vodka (optional)
Lime wedges

Mix together juices and add vodka if desired. Serve in a chilled glass with a wedge of lime over ice. Squeeze the lime into the juice for extra tartness.

Serving suggestions: This juice cocktail is a refreshing pop of color at summer parties. Serve in mason jars, highball glasses, or any unusual glassware.

Note: The original Sea Breeze recipe is thought to have originated in the 1920s, possibly at The Savoy hotel in London. Made with gin, apricot brandy, grenadine, and lemon juice, it was quite different.

BAY BREEZE COOLER (OR HAWAIIAN SEA BREEZE)

3 oz. cranberry juice drink
3 oz. pineapple juice
1 oz. vodka (optional)
Lime wedges

Similar to the Sea Breeze, the Bay Breeze packs a cool tropical punch. Mint makes a refreshing garnish.

Of course, always drink responsibly and don't drive and drink.

ABOUT THE AUTHOR

JAN MORAN is a *USA Today* and a *Wall Street Journal* bestselling author of romantic women's fiction. A few of her favorite things include a fine cup of coffee, dark chocolate, fresh flowers, laughter, and music that touches her soul. She loves to travel, and her favorite places for inspiration are those rich with history and mystery and set against snowy mountains, palm-treed beaches, or sparkly city lights. Jan is originally from Austin, Texas, and a trace of a drawl still survives, although she has lived in Southern California near the beach for years.

Her books are also available as audiobooks, and many have been translated into other languages, If you enjoyed this book, please consider leaving a brief review online for your fellow readers where you purchased this book or on Goodreads or Bookbub.

To read Jan's other historical and contemporary novels, visit JanMoran.com. Join her VIP Readers Club mailing list and her Facebook Readers Group to learn of new releases, sales, and contests.

Made in United States
Cleveland, OH
13 July 2025

18523899R00135